GENESIS

HARRY STARKE THE EARLY YEARS BOOK 1

BLAIR HOWARD

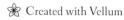 Created with Vellum

DEDICATION

This one is for Jo
As Always

1

I t was one of those wild nights in late November. The driving rain hammered the roof of the Maxima. The wipers banged back and forth smearing water across the windshield: a mini tsunami that swished first one way and then the other. I leaned forward over the wheel and squinted out into the blackness, struggling desperately to keep the car on the road.

Chattanooga in winter is always a nightmare, but this was a particularly hard storm and only the lightning that lit up the road every now and then provided any relief from the strain of driving in such a mess. I should have had the wipers replaced months ago, but I say that every time there's a storm.

The car slowed, veered to the right as it hit deep water.

I'd be better off in a frickin' boat, I thought, as I dragged the car back into the center of the road.

The white lines on the side of the road were inundated, six inches under water. The broken yellow line at the center appeared and disappeared with each gust. I should have pulled over and waited it out, but patience never was my forte. Anyway, it wasn't my first time driving that route; I'd driven it so many times I could do it with my eyes closed... *Sure you can, you dopey SOB.*

Any other time in such weather I'd have taken a cab, or an Uber, but there was a nurse's convention in town and availability, like the visibility, was zero. Those nurses have no problems dealing with people with their guts spilling out, but ask 'em to walk a city block in the rain, even with an umbrella, and they'd laugh at you. Besides, the cabbies would much rather grab those fares than my grumpy ass. Oh yeah, I'd called, but the dispatcher told me the wait would be at least an hour and a half before they could get to me. Screw that. As I said, I don't have that kind of patience.

A small branch splatted across the windshield, startling me enough to make me swerve a little; again, the tires slammed into the deep water at the side of the road, slowing the car, dragging it even further to the right as I fought the wheel. I let up on the gas and dragged the heavy car back onto the center of the lane. It was no weather to be driving and I should have known better, told Ronnie, "No, not tonight."

I'd been having a quiet night all to myself. The condo was warm and dry, and that's where I should have stayed. But my curiosity had gotten the better of me.

I had my feet up on the coffee table, NCIS on the TV, a double-decker burger with fries from Maxi's half eaten, and a glass of Heineken still untouched when my iPhone buzzed.

I picked it up, flipped the lock screen, and growled, "Yeah, Ronnie, what do you want?"

"Harry, you need to get down here—"

"Whoa!" I interrupted him. "What's up?"

"It's poker night, damn it. We need another player, and you're it."

Ronnie Hall was a long-time friend of mine. I'd known him for more than sixteen years, since before he'd gotten out of high school. He's smart, really smart. He won a scholarship to the London School of Economics where he earned a master's degree in finance, and his idea of putting that education to good use was... Well, there were few things Ronnie loved more than making money, especially when it involved playing poker.

"I'm at the Sorbonne," he said. "Come on."

I groaned. Ronnie went to the Sorbonne every Wednesday hoping for a hot game and trying to hustle whatever new kid walked through the door looking for a challenge. Sad thing is, he's not that good. I do enjoy watching him get his ass handed to him, sometimes.

The Sorbonne? It's not what you think. It's a classy name for a sleazy "night club," and I call it that with deep reservations. It is, in fact, a less-than-lovely den of ill repute, the last refuge of every low-life that can afford the price of a watered drink... and for many of Chattanooga's fashionable elite who enjoy slumming and... even mingling—yeah, that's my polite way of saying it.

The joint, to use the vernacular of the forties—not

that I'm old enough to remember such verbiage, but I do watch a lot of movies—is owned by one Benny Hinkle, a fat little bastard who would steal the watch from your wrist without you ever knowing it was gone.

"Nah, I don't think so, Ronnie. Not tonight. It's storming and—"

"Awe come on, Harry. There are new faces at the table, but there aren't enough people to play. I need you, man."

"What about Laura?"

"No, it's busy in here tonight, so she's working. Must be the weather. Come on, Harry. These two kids are guaranteed to be easy marks."

It was always hard to resist poker night with Ronnie. He's a funny guy, and fun to watch. The Sorbonne? Yeah, I even enjoyed that too. I'd spent many a night there working the job and even though the music was loud and inevitably awful and the drinks even worse, I somehow felt at home there. Yeah, I know: crazy, but true...

And I still spend more time there than I probably should. My excuse? I like to keep up with what's going on in this fair city's underworld, and there's no place I know where I can do that better than the Sorbonne, which is probably why I gave in to Ronnie's plea that dark and stormy night.

Anyway, Wednesdays always seemed to draw in a certain type of street mongrel, the ones who have nothing better to do on a Thursday morning than sleep in after a night of causing trouble. And, even though I was no longer a cop, it was, as I said, my habit to keep an eye on them.

My name, by the way, is Harry Starke. Up until a couple of months earlier, I'd been a cop, a sergeant homicide detective for the Chattanooga PD, and a damn good one, even if I do say so myself. So what happened? Well, I quit. Why did I quit? A number of reasons... the main one being one too many run-ins with the Chief of Police, a martinet named Wesley Johnston; an arrogant SOB if ever there was one.

Another reason: I never was much of a team player, and office politics... you can have 'em. And besides, it wasn't like I needed the money so, finally, I told him to take his job and shove it... More than ten years on the job, a Master's degree in Forensic Psychology from Fairleigh Dickinson, and once again I was at a loose end... Not!

The shadow crossed in front of the car so fast I didn't have time to stop. I hit the brakes hard and swerved into the mud at the side of the road.

Looking out through the deluge, it was difficult to make out the figure coming towards the driver's window, but as it came closer I could see it was a girl, just a kid.

Instinctively, my hand went for my gun and rested on the grip as she approached. Her hair, dark, bobbed, was plastered to her head and face. The raccoon eye shadow smeared above her eyes had run in rivulets down her cheeks. And she looked scared, really scared, that much was obvious.

What the hell is she doing out here alone in this kind

of weather? I thought as I rolled down the window a half-inch.

"Get in the back," I yelled at her, and I flipped the lock so she could open the door.

Okay, so I'm a little protective of my car and didn't want the front seat ruined. She was soaking wet, shivering like a newborn puppy. I cranked up the heater.

"There's a towel and a blanket on the floor back there," I said over my shoulder. "Get yourself dried off."

She did. I could hear her teeth chattering over the noise of the hot air blowing out of the heater vents.

"What the hell were you doing out there in this mess?"

"My car broke down."

I sighed and shook my head; she'd just lied to me. It wasn't just the way she said it, but I knew. There were no cars on the road a mile in either direction, not back the way I'd come nor in the mile we'd traveled since I'd picked her up; I would have noticed.

"Not got Triple A?" I asked, looking at her in the rearview mirror.

She didn't answer, but the look on her face said it all. Her lies weren't getting her anywhere with me and she knew it.

"Where are you going?" she asked.

Her voice was soft, refined, and didn't match her disheveled appearance. A flash of lightning momentarily lit up her face and she squinted: she looked older than I'd first thought. Her pretty face was drawn with stress and streaked with ruined makeup. I figured her to be around twenty-one, twenty-two, and on her own.

Why do these kids wear that black crap around their eyes and on their fingernails? I thought, staring out through the windshield and the rain. *It makes them look so hard.*

"Where are *you* going?" I said, glancing up at the rearview mirror.

She shrugged, wiped her eye with the back of her hand, streaking the black crap even further. Then she took a deep breath, closed her eyes, shook her head and said, so quietly I could barely hear it, "Wherever you're going, I suppose."

"You sure? I'm going to the Sorbonne. It's a bar. You know it?"

She didn't answer.

"I'll take you there, and you can have someone come and get you."

Her eyes looked down at the floor and then out the side window. She seemed to be deep in thought.

She finally spoke, "Yes, I know it, and that will be fine... thank you."

2

I parked on the street in front of the Sorbonne. We ran through the rain to the front door, shaking the drops off of our coats like a couple of dogs as we stepped into the... not light, that's for sure: dim? Yeah, and frickin' noisy: the jukebox was blasting out some weird, modern country music song—and I use the words lightly—by some faux cowboy I'd never heard of.

Geez, I thought, as I looked around, *no matter how many times I step into this... snake pit, I never get used to it; the smell of stale beer and even staler—is that a real word?—cigarettes hitting my nostrils like a punch in the nose.*

Ronnie was seated at a round table in a darkened corner—yeah, it was even darker—at the far end of the long barroom, along with a couple of wannabe poker sharks that I figured had probably learned their craft watching the World Series of Poker on TV. Both of them were young, both wore glasses. There was an empty chair waiting for me.

Gambling is illegal in Tennessee, but that didn't stop the regulars. Nor did it bother Benny Hinkle... Well, not much. He kept his joint quiet and we cops gave him a little space, easement, if you will. I'd learned more about Chattanooga's seedy side in that bar... And Benny, though not an official CI—confidential informant—was never averse to a little quid pro quo. He was one of my go-tos when I needed "the word on the street."

I slapped the kid on the shoulder, told her goodbye and to be careful, and I left her to make her call and headed over to the table, wrenching my wet jacket from my shoulders and shaking it to get rid of the excess water as I went. The pool cues were all being used so I hung it on the empty rack in the hope that it might dry out a little: it was right under a vent that was piping lukewarm air down from the ceiling, too cool for it to be any good when it snowed but good enough maybe to dry out my coat.

"It's about time," Ronnie said, impatiently, as I untucked my shirt and pulled the hem over the M&P9 on my hip.

"I got a little sidetracked."

The words had barely left my mouth when the kid appeared at the table. Seeing her in the light really showed the wear and tear from the storm. She must have been out there for an hour or more. Her face was pale, and she looked about ready to collapse. Ronnie checked her out.

"This is what sidetracked you?" he asked. "You better sit down, kid, before you fall down. You... want to play?"

Oh you've gotta be kidding me, Ronnie, I thought, shaking my head in amazement. *Have you no shame?*

She nodded, grabbed a chair, and squeezed herself into the small space between me and the scrawny kid on my right. The wad of cash she pulled from her pocket was wet, but she flattened it out, a stack of twenties a half-inch thick, and placed it on the table in front of her.

Laura, Benny's "partner" and barkeep appeared at my side and set down a shot of whiskey and a beer on the table in front of me. I stared at it, picked it up, and sniffed it. It was scotch, not the watered-down crap Benny usually served—Laura knew better than that—but it sure as hell wasn't the Laphroaig I was used to either. I smiled up at her and handed over a damp five-dollar bill.

She winked at me and said, "I see you have a little friend with you, Harry. What would you like, sweetie?"

"Coffee, please."

Laura let out a hearty laugh. "Oh really? You think this is Starbucks? If you want booze, we got booze. That's it."

The kid chewed on her lip and then said confidently, "A shot of tequila... Gold."

"That's more like it. Anybody else?"

"You know what I want." Ronnie, married though he was, was a harmless flirt, and she knew it.

"Yeah, tell it to someone who wants it too."

Laura sauntered off with the usual swing of her hips and Ronnie shook his head, wistfully.

Everyone thought Laura had something going on with her boss, Benny. Not true. It was all an act. She was happily married with two kids and a loving husband. The act was for tips, and to keep the clientele coming in which, in turn, made Benny a very happy man. It was a match made in... Oh yeah, but it was still fun to watch her wiggle as she walked through the crowd.

"So," Ronnie said, shuffling the cards. "Ante up. Five-dollar buy-in. Texas Hold 'Em."

We all tossed our cash into the center of the table as Ronnie flicked cards around to us.

"How old are you, kid, really?" I asked. "And what's your name?"

One, I was worried she might not be old enough to drink and two, I figured if she was going to lose her money to us, the least we could do was call her by her name.

"Phoebe. Phoebe Marsh, and I'm twenty-one."

Ronnie stopped in mid-deal at the mention of her name and stared at her with his mouth open. It wasn't a good look for a guy who prided himself on his intelligence.

The kid shifted uncomfortably in her chair and lifted the corner of her cards to give them a peek. Her eyes stayed down, and she shifted again.

There was something that the two of them knew that no one else at the table did, but I was sure Ronnie would tell me when he could. I scooped up my two cards and shielding them with a hand, fanned them out; I had a two of diamonds and a nine of spades, crap.

"Fold," I said and flung the cards face down on top of the money pile.

Ronnie smirked as he lifted them and straightened the bunch into a new pile next to the deck. Everyone else stayed in and Ronnie dealt the flop cards: nine of hearts... queen of clubs... nine of diamonds. *Crap!*

First hand and I'd tossed three of a kind, and right then I knew I was in for a rough evening.

Laura brought a second shot of tequila and set it down in front of Phoebe on a little white paper napkin. What the... I didn't even know this joint had napkins.

"What's up with the fancy service?" I asked.

"It's from the guy over there." Laura nodded her head in the direction of a shady looking guy sitting at the far end of the bar. His back was towards the front door so all I could see was his profile. Big nose, broken at least once, stubbly chin and a pronounced forehead. The tiny slit where his mouth should be was barely visible. He looked like he was in pretty good physical shape, but the face was that of a thug.

The girl looked down at the napkin and shuddered. That same look she'd had in the back seat of my car had returned, and it was clear that this character had something to do with it. She raised her cards and upped the bid made by the scrawny kid to my right. If she had a good hand, you could only tell by the money she wagered. The kid had a terrific poker face.

I'm not sure why, but something inside of me clicked. *This kid needs a friend.*

"Hey Laura, can you bring a damp bar towel so

Phoebe can clean up her face?" I smiled at the girl, trying to reassure her that somebody had her back.

"Sure. Just give me a minute."

Phoebe smiled. It seemed like she wasn't used to people being kind to her.

"I got nothing," the scrawny kid next to me said as he threw down his cards. He took out a small notebook and wrote something.

"You wouldn't be counting cards, would you?" Ronnie asked.

"No," scrawny said. "I'm calculating odds."

"A man after my own heart," Ronnie said. "What's your name?"

The scrawny kid put a finger to his glasses and shoved them back up the bridge of his nose. "Tim Clarke."

There was no way that scrawny kid was old enough to be in this joint, I'd bet my badge on it, if I still had one. But like I said before, all it takes is a little green in the right pocket to overlook little misdeeds like serving underaged kids. And this one... well, if he was even seventeen years old, my uncle was the proverbial monkey.

Ronnie laid down the turn card—ace of hearts—and upped the bet. Phoebe and the other kid matched. He turned up the river card—ace of clubs. The kid folded. It was now just Phoebe and Ronnie. The two of them were a good match, him with his indomitable attitude and her with her casual demeanor.

Laura came back, setting the towel on the table next

to Phoebe's cards and placed a small green glittery bag on top of it.

"I'm sure you'll find something in there that will make those gorgeous eyes pop," she said, gifting her with a smile and a gentle pat on the back. Then she was away, cursing and swearing at two guys who'd put their beer glasses on the pool table.

Laura had a big heart and had made sure the water on the towel was warm. You could see the steam rising from it and how happy it made Phoebe to touch it to her face.

Damn! I thought. *Whoever's been messing with this kid has really done her psyche some damage.*

Out of the corner of my eye, I noticed that the man at the bar had disappeared. His glass was empty and the coat that had been hanging over the back of his chair was gone.

"Call," Phoebe said.

Ronnie smiled as he laid down a pair of kings. "Two pair, kings and aces. Your turn." He raised his eyebrows.

"Three of a kind," she said, turning over a pair of queens.

The smirk on her face was priceless as she raked in the money and began to straighten out the bills. But that wasn't the only priceless face at the table. Ronnie was in shock. He hadn't lost a hand that big for a long time and losing—especially to a... little girl—well, it hurt.

"Excuse me for a minute," she said in a small voice as she stood up, grabbing the green case and walking around the table towards the back of the bar.

"You are coming back, right?" Ronnie said, standing up politely, his tall, slender frame towering over her as she walked by. "I'd like a chance to win back my money."

"I'm just going to pee. You'll get your chance." A crooked smile parted her pale lips and there was a spring in her step that hadn't been there earlier. Ain't it amazing what one little win in life can do for a person's confidence? She looked back over her shoulder as she headed down the hall to the bathroom and smiled.

"You want to play one without her?" I asked.

I was ready to leave. The three of a kind—my three of a kind—was indeed a warning. If I'd kept it, I would have lost my ass to Phoebe. And then, considering the sickening weather outside and the crappy drinks inside, I had an irresistible yearning for the warmth and comfort of my condo and a little twelve-year-old scotch.

"Ronnie," I said, "I'll play a couple more hands, and then I'm going to head for home."

"You just got here, damn it." Ronnie was already shuffling the deck and dishing out cards.

"You have enough players without me, and I can't see the little lady stopping any time soon."

Ronnie won the round, dealt another hand, and by the end of the second hand, the two kids were finished. They'd pretty much been cleaned out of every penny in their pockets along with whatever small amount of ego resided behind those plastic-framed glasses.

Both hands had gone long, and I was becoming worried about our friend in the bathroom. She'd left her money on the table next to her untouched drink and the now cold bar towel. Laura came up with another round of drinks for Ronnie and me.

"Where's your little friend?" she asked.

"In the bathroom. Would you mind checking on her? She's been in there for a while."

"I hope she didn't run off with my makeup bag. That douchebag at the end of the bar stiffed me already. I'd hate to lose my favorite eye shadow too." She had started to leave the table when I grabbed her arm.

"Are you talking about that ugly guy with a big nose and no mouth?"

"Yeah. You know him?"

I suddenly had a really bad feeling that something was wrong. I didn't often have such feelings, but when I did, I always trusted them and I was rarely wrong.

I pushed back my chair and headed to the back of the bar and the ladies' restroom. I knocked and without waiting, pushed open the door. There were only two stalls, both of them empty.

I heard the rear exit door of the bar clang shut and I spun around, ran to the door, grabbed the quick release bar and pushed. The door stuck.

I held the bar down and hit the door with my shoulder. It swung open and I almost fell out into the street: I was just in time to see a pair of feet being pulled into the side of a black van. The tires squealed, spun, burned rubber, and it slewed out of the parking lot even before the door slammed shut.

No plates, damn it. That figures, I thought as I pulled my M&P9 from its holster and ran out into the rain. But I was too late. All I could do was stand there and watch as the back end of the van lost traction, skidded, its tires squealing as it disappeared around the corner.

Damn! I thought. *What the hell was that about? What did the kid do that they'd go to so much trouble to grab her... and where the hell are they taking her?*

My shirt and pants were soaked. I shook my head, frustrated, slid the weapon back into its holster, and headed back through the door, past the restrooms, into the main room of the bar. The two scrawny kids were heading out the front door, having left Ronnie pouting at the table.

"What do you expect when you take all their cash so quick?" I said as I dropped into my seat.

"You're all wet," he said. "What happened? Where's Phoebe?"

"Gone."

"Good, she left my money." Ronnie reached across the table.

I grabbed his hand. "I'll hold it for her," I said.

Ronnie cocked his head and gave me a boyish grin. "She's coming back then?"

"I doubt it. Someone grabbed her, and I'm betting it was that gnarly dirtbag that was sitting at the end of the bar."

I scooped up the kid's money, and as I did, I noticed the napkin under the kid's shot glass. I moved the glass and picked up the square. There was a symbol drawn on it with an eyeliner pencil along with a phone number.

What the hell is that? I thought. *What does it mean?*

The kid must have done it when my attention was on the game. I turned it over and read the words scrawled on the other side. They were written with a blue pen. "Time to come home." The dirtbag at the bar had sent her a message.

So that's what it's about, I thought. *She's a runaway.*

"Ronnie," I said. "That funny look on your face when she told us her name... You knew who the kid was. You want to tell me how come?" I asked.

"You don't know?" he asked, his eyes wide.

I shook my head, waiting for an answer.

"Geez, Harry. Have you been hiding under a rock since you left the force? Phoebe Marsh is Frank Marsh's daughter."

And then I got it. "The guy who just went to prison for that Ponzi scheme?"

"The very same."

Marsh had stolen a boatload of money from an even bigger boatload of people and in so doing had made a boatload of enemies. Some of those enemies traveled in very bad circles, and I had no doubt that most of them wanted revenge.

Geez. The kid's in big trouble.

I took out my iPhone and dialed the number on the napkin. It rang six times and then went to voicemail.

A frickin' laundromat? What the hell is that about?

I hung up. Suds and Duds. I knew that place. It wasn't exactly what you'd think it was.

"I need to go, Ronnie," I said, getting up from the table.

"Where are you going?"
"To do a little laundry."

3

I t was still raining when I got outside. I stood for a
moment on the porch, fumbling with my car keys
in my jacket pocket. They slipped out of my hand
and landed in a puddle.

Oh great, I thought savagely. *There goes two hundred
bucks to get another fob to unlock the beast. I just knew it
wasn't going to be my night.*

I squinted and stepped out into the wind and rain.
The raindrops pummeled my face, stinging harder than a
slap by a pretty girl.

I bent down, fished the keys out of the water, and
pushed the unlock button. Sure enough: nothing.

I stuck the key into the lock and turned it... and the
frickin' alarm sounded. *Crap!* Don't you hate it when it
does that?

I scrambled in behind the wheel, stuck the key into
the ignition, shut the alarm off, and fired up the motor.

The car hummed as the rain pounded on the roof. I

tapped the screen on my phone and the Bluetooth connected.

"Call Kate."

"Calling Kate Gazzara's cell."

Detective Sergeant Kate Gazzara—yeah, she was still a sergeant back then—was my partner on the force and a force to be reckoned with herself. I was hoping she could give me a hand with Phoebe's kidnapping—well what I thought was a kidnapping. Seeing the note though, "It's time to come home," I was beginning to have my doubts. Still, I figured I should follow up, just in case.

After a couple of rings, she picked up.

"What do you want? I'm in the middle of something."

"Nice to talk to you too. Hot date?"

Kate and I had been dating for quite a while. She's stunning, a classic beauty, almost six feet tall and in amazing shape: slender, dirty blonde hair and a smile... Well, you get the idea.

"Bubble bath," she said. "I haven't had one in a year, but I finally managed to carve out a few minutes of peace... and then you called. So what *do* you want, Harry?"

The thought of her naked in the tub was more than a distraction.

"Do you know who Phoebe Marsh is, Kate?"

"Of course I do. Who doesn't?"

"I don't... didn't, not until tonight anyway. What's the scoop with her and her dad? They get along?"

She didn't answer.

"Hello?" I said.

"Sorry. I was taking a sip of wine. What was your question?"

Damn! I thought. *Are you serious?*

Normally, she'd be all over me, asking questions and poking around, wanting to know why I was being nosey, but she was either giving me the cold shoulder or she just didn't care. Something was up, and I wanted to know what it was.

"Phoebe Marsh? What is it with her and her dad? Do they get along, or what?"

"How the heck should I know? He's in jail, I know that, and I know that she's his only kid. That's about it. Maybe you should watch the news once in a while."

"Come on now, Kate. You know what that's like. I need answers from someone who knows—"

"Then call your dad," she interrupted me, "and ask him about Phoebe's father. I'm sure he can fill you in."

What the hell? Who the hell kicked her cat, I wonder?

"Are you mad at me, Kate?"

Silence.

"Okay. What did I do?"

"Why don't you check the calendar on your iPhone and call me back." Kate hung up.

Uh oh! What have I missed?

Technology doesn't scare me, but I do prefer to keep track of my appointments on paper, in a book. That way they don't accidentally get deleted and hackers can't access my private info. My spiral-bound calendar lives on the desk in my office at the condo, but I hadn't checked it in days. I didn't need to; I didn't work anymore.

I shook my head, wondering if maybe she'd put something into the calendar on my phone. If she had, it was her bad. She knew I never look at the damn thing, not even to check the date.

I pulled the car over in a Dollar General parking lot and grabbed my iPhone, opened up the calendar and... Oh crap, there it was.

I closed my eyes, but in my mind's eye, all I could see were those huge hazel eyes looking reproachfully back at me. I'd screwed up again. We'd been seeing each other for almost eight years and were both comfortable enough with the relationship... but lately, my constant screw-ups had been kinda stretching things... just a little.

Damn it, I thought. *It's her birthday.*

"Call Kate," I said, quietly, feeling like shit.

The phone rang several times and then went to voicemail. I tried again.

"Call Kate."

Come on... come on... answer the friggin' thing. But she didn't.

Oh well, I thought, *I guess I should let her cool off. I'll send her flowers and maybe she'll talk to me tomorrow.*

In the meantime, I had a visit to make.

4

S uds and Duds was a little north of 23rd on Dodds in the armpit between Fort Cheatem and Ridgedale. I call it the armpit because of the way the highway loops around Missionary Ridge like a Little League Pitcher throwing a curveball. Not the friendliest place in the city, but that didn't bother me... Well, not when I was a cop. Now? Maybe a little.

I eased the pistol out of its holster, made sure there was one in the chamber... not that I needed to; I kept the weapon ready to fire at all times, force of habit. Forget what you've seen on TV; if you get into trouble, there's never time enough to rack the slide, aim, and fire. That's the quickest way to get dead I know.

I knew Suds and Duds from my days on the force. It was a hangout for drug dealers, gang bangers, and folks who wanted to grab a fix and do the wash at the same time.

As I drove, I thought about the paper napkin.

Although the phone number rang the S&D business, Phoebe's drawing, symbol or whatever it was, wasn't their logo. There's was cheesy—a basket of dirty drawers with bubbles rising above it.

Phoebe's drawing was pretty rough, hard to make sense of. *A series of circles with points, interlaced, one inside the other*, I pictured it in my mind... What it might represent, I had no idea... Or maybe it meant nothing—just a doodle, the product of the active imagination of a rich kid with a bob cut and black nail polish. That didn't seem likely though. She drew that picture and left it next to her money for a reason.

Was it her way of telling me that she knew they were after her and if they took her, she hoped I'd come looking for her? It was one hell of a stretch, but there was only one way to find out: I had to find her.

I found a parking spot on the street under a bright light a block away from the laundromat. Not that the light would stop the bangers from stripping my car, but it was better than the dark spots down in front of the washeteria where every other car was a piece of garbage compared to mine.

What is it they say? *Thieves always steal from the neighbor with the best stuff.* So I found a spot between an '05 Lexus and an '07 Corvette. I figured if there was any stripping to be done, they'd go for one of those instead of mine. Well, I hoped so.

I locked the car using the button on the armrest, stepped out into the rain, pulled the collar of my jacket up around my neck, and headed down the street to the laundromat on the corner.

"Hey buddy, you got a buck?"

"What?"

I stopped, turned, and looked at the guy lying in the doorway of a store that looked as if it had been closed since before Pontius was a pilot. He looked cold and hungry. The pile of dirty blankets he was lying on was sopping wet, and he'd piled sheets of cardboard, flattened boxes, on top of himself to try and keep dry whatever small part of him he could. It wasn't often I'd fork over money to a vagrant, but this guy looked half dead. Even so, there was no way I was going to fish out my wallet in this neighborhood. I did, however, have a stray five in my jacket pocket that made its way into his hand. He was oh so grateful.

Hugging the wall and overhangs from doorway to doorway, I finally made it to the bright lights on the corner —I jest, of course. The lights were indeed bright, but the place was a pigpen: sleazy, dirty, where hard-looking women in too-tight pants chewed gum while they waited for their panties fluffing in the dryers. In a neighborhood like that, a laundry stop was more of a dating service for losers looking for drugs and... cheap sex.

I knew I was out of place, but I needed answers. The bell jingled as I walked through the door. It was crowded for a Wednesday night. There was a trashy-looking couple in one corner shooting up and a young woman, just a kid of maybe eighteen or nineteen, bouncing a baby on her knee while checking the messages on her phone. *Geez. Babies having babies.*

A black kid seated on a stool in the corner looked like he might be a refugee from the weather. He wasn't doing laundry; he was reading a comic book, *Hellboy*. I had to stop myself from shaking my head. I didn't know him, but I knew the type.

"Hey, kid," I said. "Do you know a chick named Phoebe?"

He didn't look up from his book. "Hey kid..." That's when I noticed the wires dangling from his ears. I tugged on one and out popped the bud.

"What the...? What do you want, old man?"

Old man? Geez!

It took everything I had not to smack the kid upside his head.

"Do you know a girl named Phoebe?"

The look that crawled across his face told me he did.

"Naw. Never heard of her." He put the bud back into his ear and looked down at the comic book pretending to read it.

I grabbed the wire again and jerked the bud out of his ear, taking the iPod with it.

"Hey, asshole, give it back!" He half stood, reaching for it.

I took a step backward.

"She was grabbed by some grungy looking guy," I said, dangling the iPod in front of him, "big head, no mouth. You know him?"

The kid looked around nervously. "Gimme it." He

raised his hand, about to make another grab for it. "I don't want no trouble..." His voice trailed off as he looked past me over my shoulder.

I turned around just in time to get punched in the nose.

HE WAS BIG. I'm talking enormous, a frickin' Goliath. At six-two and two hundred and fifteen pounds I'm no slouch, but this guy looked like the Empire State Building towering over the tourists. He swung at me again, but the punch was slow and easy to dodge. I sidestepped and threw a punch of my own into his gut. My fist sank in deep. The Pillsbury Doughboy had nothing on this guy. His belly was a never-ending well of flab and blubber. Spit and chewing tobacco came flying out of his mouth and all over my face. *How the hell can anybody stand that stuff?*

Quicker than you could blink, my gun was in my hand and jammed up into his nostrils. His eyes widened into two white onions and he snorted snot all over the barrel of the gun. I tapped him with it on the bridge of his nose, wiped the crap off the muzzle on the collar of his shirt, then jammed it back up his nose.

"You're going die young if you keep chewing on that garbage—if the fat doesn't kill you first," I told him, wiping the blood from my own nose with the back of my hand.

The kid behind me jumped to his feet and tried to

scramble past me and out of the door, but my other hand reached for his collar and anchored him in place. He was going nowhere.

"What's up with you two?" I asked. "I just need answers to a few questions about Phoebe."

The place by then had gone completely quiet, except for the hum of the rotating machines. The big guy suddenly came to life, took me by surprise, exploded into action, slammed the gun to one side, then spun around and ran out of the laundry followed by most of the people waiting for clothes, all of them leaving their goodies in the washers and dryers.

Boy, I thought, *I never would have believed he could move that fast.*

Phoebe, so it seemed, was some kind of plague, and the mere mention of her name struck fear into anyone that heard it. I was now certain there was something going on, and even more certain I was going to find out what it was.

"Look, kid, I'm a Private Investigator..." Where the hell that came from, I had no idea, but it *sounded good.* "And I need to find her, Phoebe. She's in trouble and needs help. Now, what can you tell me?"

"Private Eye?" He was astounded. "You kiddin' me? Don't even think about it. They'll take you out so fast you'll think it's still yesterday... Private Eye? Really? No shit?"

"Yeah, really. Now tell me. What the hell's going on?"

"You's already dead, man. They got an army an'

they'll chew you up, no matter who you is or what you do."

There are few things in life that I enjoy more than a challenge—a good Scotch and taking down bad guys are at the top of my list—but there's nothing I like better than proving people wrong.

"You think?" I said, grabbing his arm. "Come on, kid. We're going to Denny's and you can tell me more about this army."

I dragged him out of the laundromat. The rain had let up a little, which was a relief after the beating it had given me earlier. We didn't say much on the walk to the car, but I did manage to pry a name out of the kid.

"My name's Stitch." "What kind of a name is Stitch? Is it a nickname?"

"No, I was born with it. What kind of a name is Harry? Sounds like you need a shave or sumpin'."

I shoved him into the passenger seat and slammed the door. I rounded the front of the car, watching him through the windshield, hoping he wouldn't make a run for it. He didn't.

I got in behind the wheel, fired up the engine, and turned right onto Dodds. I glanced at the kid—he looked terrified; it was time to get serious. I opened my mouth to speak, but he beat me to it.

"Hey, man. You tryin' to get us both killed? These guys mean business, man. Look, I love Phoebe, but you're not doing her no favors by goin' lookin' for her."

"Well we're not doing her any favors leaving her to those thugs," I said. "She was scared to death running around in the rain tonight trying to get away from someone. What was she scared of, Stitch? Who was she running away from?"

The kid just stared at me like I was speaking another language.

"Come on. If you really love Phoebe..."

He shook his head and looked down at his lap. "I can't. They'll kill me if I rat 'em out. They don't care about anyone or anything, least of all me. An' my dad—"

"I won't let anyone hurt you... Your dad? What's it got to do with him? Who is he? What's his name?"

"Lester Tree. He kinda runs things aroun' here. They call him Shady."

Shady freakin' Tree... I thought, stunned by the mere thought of him. *Well if that doesn't just beat all.*

I just couldn't imagine that crooked piece of garbage having children. It was harder still to imagine that anyone would want to breed with the slime-ball, but my guess was there'd been a lot of lying and huge quantities of drugs and alcohol involved. No wonder the kid was freaked out.

"That sucks, Stitch," I said. "I'm sorry to hear it." And I truly meant it.

"Yeah, well, we can't choose our parents."

Geez, ain't that the truth.

I got lucky growing up in a normal house with caring folks. This poor kid... geez. It didn't get any worse than Shady Tree. The guy was a grifter with a passion for concocting stories and schemes that would make a nun blush. His looks were deceiving: he was tall, handsome, well built, wore his hair in dreads, and most of the time he wore a blue do-rag wrapped around his head. His game was anything lowball. He cared nothing for the law and would do anything shy of murder to make a buck.

"So what is it with these guys?" I asked. "Drugs, human trafficking, prostitution? Why are they so interested in Phoebe?"

"Her old man, of course. That dude be bad, man, everythin' every street mugger aspires to be, 'cept in prison."

"So what about your dad, is he in on it?"

"Shady? Hah. No way, man. That be way outa his league."

"I still don't get it about Phoebe? She's just a kid. Why is she so important?"

"Her dad was goin' down, for a long time. I heard he sold her to some dudes; not for money, for protection while he be in the slammer."

Holy cow... He sold her? What kind of man... Shit, he sure as hell isn't gonna win a Father of the Year award.

I got it. I shook my head and said, "So trafficking then, forced prostitution? Talk to me about the dudes he sold her to. Where do they keep the kids?" I asked, as I pulled into the Denny's lot and parked close to the building.

"I don't know. I used to, but they don't trust me no more."

I took the napkin from my pocket and showed him the drawing. "Do you recognize this?"

There was a sharp intake of breath, then he said, "Where you git that?"

"Phoebe drew it before she was kidnapped. We were playing poker at the Sorbonne and some gnarly guy with a small mouth and a big forehead sent the napkin over with this message." I turned over the napkin to reveal "It's time to come home" and the kid bit his lip.

"That's how I got to Suds & Duds. Phoebe wrote the number on the back. What does it mean?"

Stitch wiped his mouth with his sleeve and looked out the car window. "I can't, man. They'll know I told you and kill me. The big guy in the laundry-mat—there's a whole bunch just like him. He only ran away because he thought you were a cop, but he be back by now and looking for me. They watch me all the time. I promised them I wouldn't say nothin'. If they find out I did..."

He opened the car door and started to get out. I couldn't let him get away without telling me where she was.

"Stitch, please..." I said.

He shook his head. "I gotta go."

It happened so fast I didn't see it coming. I heard the sharp crack of a suppressed gun and the kid's head slammed back into the car door jamb and he collapsed, his brains all over my car. I lurched back in my seat, then looked out through the open passenger door; the big guy from the laundromat was standing in the middle of the lot with a smirk on his face and a gun in his hand.

Son of a frickin' bitch. He killed the kid.

I jerked my M&P9 from its holster, opened my door

and rolled out, keeping the car between the thug and me. I could see him through the car windows, but before I could get off a shot, he and the goon that was with him took off running down the alley.

I thought about it, but I couldn't go after them. I had a dead kid slumped half in and half out of the front seat of my car.

"I'll get the son of a bitch," I promised the kid.

5

I confirmed the kid was dead and then I called 911. That done, I called Kate. It went to voicemail. *Damn it!*

"Hey, Kate, it's Harry. Look, I'm sorry about your birthday, but I need your help. I'm in the parking lot at Denny's... Kate, I'm standing here staring at a dead kid... Some damn goon just shot him, right in front of me. It's Shady's son. So, call me... please?"

She called me back almost immediately.

"Harry, what the hell's going on? I heard the call over the radio." Even when Kate was mad, she was all cop first.

"It's a long story and not a pretty one. Can you get down here? I'm betting Henry Finkle will be here any minute and you know what that means."

Assistant Chief Henry Finkle was Kate's immediate superior and, as far she was concerned, had an agenda all his own. He wanted her in his bed.

"Hang tight. I'll be there soon."

I was right about Finkle. He turned up a few minutes before Kate and chomping at the bit, hoping to find something he could hang me with, but it wasn't going to happen, not this time.

"Starke," he snapped. "What the hell's going on? You're not off the force a month and you turn up at the scene of a homicide. Get the hell out of here."

"I'm afraid not. I'm a witness."

"Aw, don't tell me you shot this kid."

Why would you even think that, Henry?

"Hell no, I didn't shoot him. You know better than that. The guy who did was a big ugly goon. Six-seven, bald, huge belly. I took a punch from him at the launderette, Suds and Duds. The dead kid is Shady Tree's son."

Finkle scratched his head and looked at me in disbelief. "Shady Tree? You're kidding, right? How do you know he was Shady's kid?"

"He told me, for Pete's sake. I was following a lead, a kidnapping and..."

"You *what?* You were following a lead? You can't do that. You're not a cop anymore. Back off and report it like any other citizen."

"He did. He reported it to me." Kate had a way of showing up just at the right time. "I asked him to look into it further. Not as a cop, but as a private investigator."

Finkle looked back and forth at us. "Phhht! A private investigator? Now I've heard it all... When the hell did that happen? Never mind, forget it, I don't want to know.

I'll have someone take your statement, then you get the hell out of here and stay the hell out of my way. Private investigator my ass... You got papers for that?"

"Working on it, Henry," I said, mentally crossing my fingers.

He shook his head, exasperated, waved a hand in the air as if he was circling the wagons, and turned away yelling. "Get forensics over here before the rain washes away all the evidence!"

The rain had started coming down again, hard. Kate and I ducked under a doorway and some newbie cop joined us, said he was supposed to take my statement. I told him okay and looked at him, waiting. He just stood there, looking uncomfortable. It turned out it was his first time. I had to feed it to him like a two-year-old. Kate was amused, but not me. It was a sad end to a really bad night.

The statement took at least an hour—okay maybe not an hour... fifteen minutes, it just seemed that long—and then the rookie shambled back to Finkle who glared at me the entire time he was being briefed.

"Come on, Harry," Kate said. "Let's go someplace where we can talk. I need to know what the hell you've been doing."

She followed me to the IHOP on Brainerd Road. It was late and, other than Budd's just across the street, it was the only place still open. We grabbed a booth in the back near the kitchen. The food actually smelled appetizing, and we browsed the menu while the waitress poured the coffee.

"Thank you," Kate smiled as the waitress huffed and

turned away. "You've been busy tonight," she said to me, her eyes on the creamer as she dumped it into the cup and stirred the swirls with a spoon.

"Just a little... Hey, I really am sorry... your birthday."

"So you had to kill a kid to make it up to me?" She smirked and added a big spoonful of sugar to her cup.

"Don't joke about it, Kate. You know I didn't kill that kid."

Kate smiled and nodded. "That I do, so don't just sit there with that stupid look on your face. Tell me what happened."

We both ordered breakfast—eggs, bacon, sausage, hash browns, and a short stack—and I told Kate about Phoebe, the mouthless man at the Sorbonne and the van, and how I thought he'd snatched her. Then I pulled out the napkin. Her eyes lit up when I handed it to her and she smiled a wry smile.

"You recognize it?"

"Maybe... It's kind of rough, the drawing, but it looks like the sign at the Rose Café on Third."

I frowned. "The Rose Café." I shook my head. "I don't know it. Should I?"

"Not sure. Vice has been watching the place for a while, but so far nothing, at least that I know of."

"Who owns it, do you know?" I asked.

"No, but it should be easy enough to find out. Are you thinking it might have something to do with your kidnapping?"

"I'm not sure it's a kidnapping. Turn it over."

"Time to come home..." she said quietly. "So the kid's a runaway, then?"

"That's exactly what I was thinking, but..."

"But you've got one of those crazy gut feelings again, right?"

"Well yeah, but it's not just that. It's also who she is... Where's home, and who wants her? Not her dad, that's for sure. You know, that kid told me Phoebe's father sold her to... hell, I don't know, not yet, but I will, for protection while he's inside. If he did, then she's in big trouble: forced prostitution. The dead kid—his name is Stitch—said something about an army. I guess he was talking about some sort of gang."

"Trafficking," she said, looking up at me over the rim of her cup. "I'm not surprised. Vice has been all over that problem for a couple of years. Nice, just what we needed around here. Did you talk to August like I suggested?"

"No, but I will. Was he involved in the Marsh case? He never mentioned it."

"I don't think so, but he's into that world. I hear the feds are about to make a move on Bernie Madoff; same deal, Ponzi scheme, though on a much bigger scale than Marsh."

"Yeah, I heard about Madoff," I said. "Who hasn't? I'll talk to August first chance I get. In the meantime, I need to find the girl."

She nodded. "So what's your plan?"

"I don't have one, but she drew that thing on the napkin for a reason. I guess I'll start with that. I'll go by the Rose Café in the morning and check it out."

"It's already morning, Harry."

The waitress came by, refilled our cups and took away our plates.

"So, how's the new partner?" I asked.

Kate shifted in her chair and gave me a sour look. I knew that look well. It was the face she made whenever she disapproved of something. Glad this time it was somebody else besides me.

"That good, huh?"

"No, he's that bad. Look, it's my birthday. Can we talk about something a little lighter?"

Almost as if she was listening in, the waitress came to the table with a piece of apple pie topped with a glowing candle. I'd managed to slip her a note along with a twenty when she took the plates, saying it was Kate's birthday and asking her to do something nice.

The waitress, singing her heart out—off-key, God bless her—set the plate of pie in front of Kate. She cocked her head, gifted me with a sideways glance, took in a breath, and gently blew out the candle.

"Okay, you're forgiven," she whispered. "Sorry I was a bitch. I thought you forgot my birthday. I didn't know you'd been dealing with this crap all night."

I didn't have the guts to tell her I forgot.

"Hurry up and finish your pie. We can go back to your place and I'll give you your present."

She knew exactly what that meant and downed the apple pie with just a couple of spoonfuls. Less than thirty minutes later we were in her apartment and everything was right with the world... for a little while at least.

I'd be some kind of a dope if I ever let this one go, I thought as I lay back and closed my eyes.

6

I woke around five-thirty the following morning, Thursday. My shoulders were sore from all the tension. They get like that now and then, especially when I'm dealing with a complex case. I rolled over and spooned Kate who groaned a little and snuggled back into me. *Mmmm, nice. I may never get out of this bed.*

I eased myself up onto my elbow and gazed down at her. Her eyelids fluttered, and I couldn't help but wonder what she was dreaming about.

The ride back to her place the previous evening was... enlightening, let's put it that way. She wanted to talk, and she did. She was running her first murder investigation as lead detective and it wasn't going well. The major problem was her new partner, and I could well understand why. I knew the guy, not well, but I'd run across him during investigations of my own. He was a vice cop then. It suited him... it suited his personality, and he was used to doing things his way.

But that wasn't all: he seemed to have an inside track to Assistant Chief Henry Finkle and that wasn't at all good. Kate didn't like to talk about it, but I knew what was going on between her and Tiny. I'd even offered to do something about it, but she was having none of that.

"If he needs a kick in the teeth," she'd said, "I'm quite capable of handing him one."

Anyway, apparently Dick Tracy—it was a nickname that had come with the job back when he was still at the Academy—had been undercover far too long and, as I said, was used to doing things his way. Detective "Dick" was also a misogynist and didn't like to be told what to do by a woman. And Kate, I promise, was and still is some kind of woman. He couldn't have run up against a tougher one and was bound to lose; she could hold her own against any man.

Even so, I felt bad for her. She loved her job and took it seriously. Nobody could match the level of commitment and honesty she brought to the force. She put a lot of pressure on herself to pick up the slack when somebody screwed up or just didn't care about what they were doing. Public servant to her meant serving the public, and she wouldn't give any less.

Her eyes opened and she looked up at me.

"You know it always wakes me up when someone's staring at me."

"Oh yeah, and how many people have been staring at you when you're sleeping?"

"Only you," she said, closing her eyes and wriggling her butt into the spoon.

I kissed her and it felt the same as it did every time
—heavenly.

"Don't go to work today," I whispered. "I'll take you
to lunch."

"Let me guess. The Rose Café."

She's a sharp one.

"Come on. It'll be like old times. The two of us,
working together again."

"You left the force, Harry. I didn't. Somebody's gotta
hold down the fort." She was barely awake but already
thinking about Tracy. "Besides, you've got a new gig."

"Oh yeah, what's that?"

"Private Investigator."

What? And she says I'm frickin' psychic.

She rose up onto her elbow, grabbed the sheet as it
fell, before... Well, you get the idea.

"Think about it, Harry," she said earnestly. "You'd be
your own boss. No Wesley Johnston forever on your ass.
It's you, Harry. Think Mike Hammer... I could be your
Velda."

"That would mean you'd have to quit your—"

"Forget it," she interrupted me. "Find some other
Velda. I'm staying put! I'll be your Captain Pat
Chambers."

"*Captain?* That'll be the day. You're just a sergeant."

"Okay, Sergeant Chambers then."

"I'd much rather you just be my Kate Gazzara." I
kissed the tip of her nose, each eyelid in turn, then her
lips.

I lay back down, my hands behind my head, and

closed my eyes. "You seem to know a lot about Mike Hammer," I said. "How come?"

"Something you don't know about me, Harry, is that I read... a lot. I love Mickey Spillane."

Hmm, I thought. *I kinda like the idea. Mike Hammer? Hah... Could be fun... I really hadn't thought about making the PI thing official—it was just a ploy to get Stitch to open up—but she may have something. I sure as hell need something to do... and this Phoebe Marsh thing might just be my way in.*

I continued to think about it... Damned if it wasn't a good idea.

"Yeah?" she asked, smiling.

"I dunno. I've never run a business before."

"Lucky that you know someone who can help."

"Terrific! You *are* gonna quit the force and come work with me?" *Would that ever be a dream come true?*

"I was talking about Ronnie, you nut. Wasn't he a business major?"

"Yeah, he was, is... Hmm, maybe I'll give him a call—"

"Later, big boy," she interrupted me. "I haven't finished with you yet."

It was almost seven when we finally rolled out of bed. We had coffee together and then went our separate ways: Kate to work and me back home to shower and change into clean clothes.

I was a mess; my rain-soaked duds had dried out overnight but were spattered with blood from my nose and half the contents of Goliath's fat mouth: speckles of chew and snot. I must have looked like I'd just crawled out of a dumpster, and I had to wonder how Kate could even stand to look at me, much less sleep with me, looking the way I did.

She called me while I was on my way to the condo. They'd found Goliath—the big dude that shot the kid. His name was Joseph—"JoJo" sometimes "JJ"—James.

He denied having anything to do with it and, of course, he had a rock-solid alibi for the time of the murder. He was at the movies with a half-dozen of his buddies. *I expected that! If nothing else, thugs are predictable.*

I parked the Maxima on the road outside the condo and, as I walked up the front steps, I noticed that the front door was open, just a crack, but it was enough to raise the hair on the back of my neck and for me to grab the Smith and Wesson from its holster. I mounted the steps, gently pushed the door open with the barrel of the gun, and took a step inside. The guy appeared out of the kitchen doorway. I had the weapon up to his face and...

"Harry," August yelped as he dropped the empty grocery bag and flung both hands in the air above his head. "It's me! Don't shoot. I was just bringing bagels."

Yeah, it was my dad. He was scared out of his brains, and I didn't blame him. Even so, a thought popped into my head: *wow, if only all those people he'd sued and taken to the cleaners could see him now.*

August Starke is one of the toughest and most honest attorneys in the business. With a tort practice that has gone after some of the biggest companies in the world, his name would bring shudders from any corporate lawyer who had to face him in a courtroom.

"You silly old man," I said, softly, stunned with the enormity of what had just happened, and the thought of what could have happened.

With pistol still in hand, I threw my arms around him and hugged him.

"Damn it, Dad! I could have killed you."

"That's enough," he said, gruffly, and pushed me away. He took a step back, brushed an imaginary speck of dirt from his shirt, picked up the bag, motioned for me to go on in, and then closed the door.

"I didn't see your car," I said, holstering the weapon. "Where is it?"

"It's parked across the street." He turned, looked at me, and said, "You're not looking so good, Harry. You should go beg Wesley Johnston to take you back. You're not cut out for the easy life. Would you like me to have a word with him for you?"

"Not in this life... or the next," I said.

He looked sharp in his usual Thursday morning golf attire: black shirt, accented by a gold chain around his neck, white slacks, and a pair of white Golfstreet shoes. He always dressed well, but today he looked particularly good.

"You playing this morning?" I asked as I followed him into the kitchen.

"Of course: nine holes with the Mayor and that new District Court Judge. I shall, as they say, take them to the cleaners."

My old man was worth more than $200 million, but he loved squeezing his pals on the golf course; never for more than ten on the match and five-dollar birdies. He said it kept them honest.

"The Bagel Shop was busy this morning," he said, "but not too busy to make your favorite breakfast sandwich—fried egg, bacon, cheese and all the grease you can handle—disgusting. How can you eat that crap, Harry?"

"Just the way Nana used to make 'em," I said as I took off my jacket and holster, hung them both on a chair at the kitchen table.

I grabbed the wrapped sandwich, peeled away the paper, held it to my nose, and inhaled the intoxicating aroma. "How the heck do they get the egg to taste so good?" I said, more to myself than to my father, as I unwrapped the rest of the sandwich.

"They use bacon grease, lots of it."

"You want to make some coffee?" I asked. "Or I can do it, if you like."

"I'll do it. Dark Italian or Breakfast?"

"Italian," I said. "Where's your oatmeal?"

"Done. Italian it is. I think I'll join you," he said. "I didn't know when you would get home, and oatmeal tastes like glue when it's cold, so coffee will do just fine."

At fifty-eight years old, my father had the body of a twenty-five-year-old. He ate the right things, worked out at least every other day, and his abs showed it. Me, I work out too, and I love to run, and I play golf now and then too, mostly with August and a couple of his friends on Saturday mornings. So, I do try to stay in shape, bacon grease aside.

"How's Rose?" I asked, and I took a bite of the sandwich.

Rose is my stepmother and an anomaly. She's twenty years younger than August—just three years older than me—and if you didn't know her, or my father, you would be forgiven for thinking she was his trophy wife. I mean, my dad was a prime catch—a rich lawyer, well-respected in the community—but that's not her at all. She loves him almost to distraction, and I love her for it... and so does August.

"She's well," he said. "Started working for some new charity this week. Something to do with kids, I think."

I nodded and took another bite of my sandwich, but my mind was beginning to wander, and he could tell.

"Where are you, Harry? What's on your mind?"

I pursed my lips, sighed through my nose, then said, "What do you know about Frank Marsh?"

He looked surprised at the question.

"He just went down for fifteen years, as I recall, some kind of Ponzi scheme. Why do you ask?"

"I ran into his daughter, Phoebe. Nice kid, but I think she might be in all kinds of trouble. Big trouble."

"She might be nice, but not Frank. He took his investors for something in excess of one hundred million and it's gone. They're looking for it, but I think it's probably a lost cause. So what's it to you?"

"Just something I'm working on."

I filled him in what had happened to Phoebe at the Sorbonne, and to the Stitch killing all without going into the gory details.

I wasn't sure I wanted to drag my father into what I knew could quickly become a huge mess. Hell, I wasn't even sure I should be digging into it, but I figured giving him the details couldn't hurt.

"So you're working the case then? That means you got your job back?" He smiled. He'd always been one to brag about his son the homicide detective, and sometimes he even had good reason to; I'd put a lot of bad guys away.

"Naw, I haven't got my old job back... Dad, I've decided to go into business for myself..." I took a deep breath and continued, "as a private investigator."

He stared wide-eyed at me for a minute, then reached across the table, grabbed my hand, squeezed it, looked me squarely in the eye, and said, "Harry, that's terrific. It's the best thing you've ever done for yourself. What can I do to help? You're going to need clients. I can help you with that. I can send a lot of business your way... I can even use you myself."

"Hey, hey, slow down," I said, laughing. I haven't even started yet; it's all still in the works. I'm thinking I might hire Ronnie..."

But he was no longer with me, not in spirit anyway. He looked at his watch. "Ronnie, huh?" he said, absently. "That's good, Harry, very good, but we'll have to talk about it later. Right now, I've got to run. Can't keep the mayor waiting, now can we?"

He looked me up and down and grimaced. "Call me later... In the meantime, you might want to shower and change your clothes. You look and smell awful." He winked, stood up, walked around the table, slapped me on the shoulder, and walked out the door.

7

I finished my sandwich and took his advice. The hot shower felt good and I lingered in the water far longer than I should have, and then... Well, the hot stream of water felt good, better than good, so I decided to follow Kate's lead. I put the stopper in the tub and added a splash of shampoo for a bubble bath. Okay, so it's not something I'd ever admit to, but it did loosen up the shoulders.

After allowing myself a half hour of peace and quiet, I decided it was time to get to work. I hauled myself out of the tub, toweled myself dry, went into the bedroom to get dressed: all black seemed the appropriate attire for my new status... and kind of my own little nod to the dead kid, Stitch. So I grabbed a pair of black jeans, a black tee, and black boots.

Stitch... I thought as I pulled on the boots. *Poor kid. If only I had listened to him and left him alone, maybe he'd still be alive... There you go again, Harry, second-guessing yourself, and you know what that's worth: not even a cup of coffee these days.*

If there's one thing I learned as a cop, it was that you can't let the crazy stuff get to you, let it haunt you. But haunt me or not, nothing was going to keep me from taking down Goliath. *I'll hunt that bastard until the day I die.*

I stood, checked myself in the mirror, turned away unimpressed, tried to shake off the black mood, unsuccessfully, made myself another cup of coffee, then went into my living room and flopped down in front of the great expanse of floor-to-ceiling windows—the main reason I bought the condo—and took in the magnificent view of the Tennessee River... beautiful, even in the rain. The surface of the water was still, broken only by the raindrops that turned the great river into a vast bed of nails.

I grabbed my laptop from the side table and opened it. I'd planned to do some research, but the view through the windows had grabbed me and wouldn't let go; intoxicating, it reminded me once again of how lucky I was to own the condo on Lakeshore Lane.

I'd gotten it at one hell of a good price, from an old duck who wanted to run off to Dove Mountain in Arizona. She claimed the dry climate there would help her bursitis. I think she even gave me a little discount on the place since I was a cop. I spent a small fortune renovating it just the way I wanted.

Finally, with pen in hand and notepad in front of me, I knuckled down and began my search for information about the Marsh case and human trafficking. Something inside me kept telling me that they—either one or both—were involved in Stitch's murder... and Phoebe's abduction. That being so, I figured a history lesson was as good a place to begin my investigation...

I am, after all, a private dick. The thought made me grin. I really was beginning to like the idea.

I tapped the keys and Googled Frank Marsh. Up popped page after page after page devoted to the case, much more information than I had time to go into in depth, but I managed to glean enough to confirm what August had told me: the man was a prime candidate for that new TV show, *American Greed.* And August was right: most of the one-hundred-three million was still missing. *There's one motive for Phoebe's kidnapping. It would be a great way to pressure Frank... if only he gave a damn.*

I moved on and Googled Human Trafficking. Again, I was gifted with more information than I could handle... *I need to find someone who can handle all this crap for me. Hmmm, that's something to think about.*

I leaned back and stared unseeing out of the great window, thinking about Shady Tree, wondering if he was involved in some way. He wasn't a killer, at least not to my knowledge. And there's no way he would have killed his own kid—but he sure as hell was involved with a lot of people that wouldn't think twice about it.

And what about that? I thought. *If somebody'd killed my kid, I'd be all over him, in a heartbeat. I need to talk to*

Shady... find out what the hell he's thinking. In the mean-time, though...

I called Ronnie. Kate's idea that I should hire him was a good one, and this was the right time for me to reel him in.

"What the hell happened to you last night?" he asked when he picked up. "It was all over the news this morning about you and a dead teen. What happened at that laundromat? Tell me you didn't get into an argument over fabric softener."

Between Ronnie and Kate, I got my fair share of ribbing.

"I was trying to find that girl, Phoebe. I found the kid at the laundromat. I was talking to him when some goon tried to warn me off, with his fist. I dealt with him and then took the kid to Denny's for a chat. Well, that was the plan, but we were just getting out of the car when the goon reappeared—he must have followed us. He just walked up and shot the kid in the face; the poor kid died on the spot."

"Geez, so then what?"

"Kate Gazzara came by and got me out from under that little rat Henry Finkle... Here's the thing though: do you remember that guy Shady Tree? I told you about him one time. It was his kid that died. I'm thinking somebody didn't want him talking to me."

"What about the goon? Did they catch him?"

"Yeah, but the fat pig had an alibi. He claimed he was watching Mary Frickin' Poppins or some other garbage at the movies. Don't worry though, I'll get the son of a bitch and make him pay, but that's not why I called you. You're not working, right?"

"Er... Right... Why d'you ask?"

"A couple things. Look, I'm at home. I have a proposition for you. Can you swing by say... now?"

The line was quiet for a minute, then, "Proposition? What proposition?"

"I'll tell you when you get here... Are you interested or not?"

"Well, yes, but I haven't had a chance to shower. Let's say in an hour: eleven... make it eleven-thirty. That okay?"

"Sure. I'll see you then."

8

I figured it would be at least an hour-and-a-half before Ronnie arrived so, rather than sit around and wait, I decided I had time to do a little recon, drive over to the Rose Café and see what I could see. I slipped into my shoulder holster, checked the weapon, holstered it, then grabbed my black leather jacket and a golf umbrella—I know, I know, but it was still raining and I sure as hell wasn't going to get drowned again.

A couple of minutes later I was out the door, in the rain and running to the car which was still parked out on the road.

It was a short drive to East Third Street. Parking was easy at that time in the morning, and I found a spot at the curb close to the front entrance of the Rose Café. Sure enough, the sign had the same flower logo as Phoebe's drawing... well, not really, but close enough. The image on the sign was a stylized white rose, à la the English Wars of the Roses.

I guess the kid embellished it a little, I thought. *No wonder Kate smiled when she saw it.*

I wasn't sure what I was looking for, or what I might find, but my gut was telling me that there was something odd about the place.

I pushed the door open and stepped inside. It wasn't exactly what I expected... if it was indeed a cover for some sort of illegal activity. It was, in fact, kind of nice, casual, with lots of wood—flat wood panels on the walls, heart pine floor, heavy wooden beams across the ceiling, and small, elegant round wooden tables with little red candles. As cafés go, it all seemed quite normal, inviting.

I grabbed a menu from beside the register and took a seat at a table off to the side by the window. As always, I sat with my back to the wall, facing the door, and with a good view out of the window. Paranoid? Better that than dead, right?

The waitress was tall and... not exactly pretty, but attractive enough, and pleasant, with orangey red hair, deep green eyes and long eyelashes that licked the top of her eyelids. I never saw anybody with eyelashes that long before. And they were real too. She had a smile that lit up the room

"Hi. Welcome to the Rose Café," she said as she set a glass of water down in front of me. "I'm Penelope. I haven't seen you around here before." She had a soft, Southern drawl, probably from one of the Carolinas.

"Hi, Penelope. Yeah, it's my first time here. What's the best thing on the menu?"

She smiled and said, "The best thing on the menu is God's love."

Uh oh, here we go, I thought.

She continued, "I can give you a giant helping of that."

"Coffee, please," I said, with a wry smile.

She smiled back at me, nodded, and walked away.

I pulled out my notepad and Phoebe Marsh's napkin, looked around, and began to make notes, trying to get a handle on the place. It wasn't working. As far as I could tell, the Rose Café was legit.

Penelope returned with my coffee and was about to set it on the table when she saw the napkin, and her hand shook, slopping coffee over the edge of the cup. The look on her face was enough to tell me she recognized the drawing. She set the coffee cup on top of the napkin and pointedly glanced up at the security camera on the ceiling in the corner of the room as if to warn me.

"Our breakfast sandwiches are to die for," she said. "I'll have the cook make you a corned beef hash and egg —*to go*," and she abruptly turned and walked away.

What was that about? I thought as I watched her retreat into the kitchen.

I took her hint, if that's what it was, and slid the napkin out from under the coffee cup and put it back into my pocket.

The breakfast sandwich from the Bagel Shop I'd eaten earlier was still weighing heavily in my gut, but I figured another one couldn't hurt, so I went back to penning notes while I waited, but my heart was no longer in it. I was trying to figure out whether Penelope was on my side or not.

The service was fast: Penelope returned with the sandwich before I'd even finished my coffee.

"I know you must be in a hurry," she said pointedly. "That'll be seven dollars even."

I could tell she wasn't going anywhere until I'd left. I dug into my pocket and fished out a ten.

"Keep it," I said as I tossed it onto the table, grabbed the breakfast sandwich, and headed for the door.

That was the first time I'd been eighty-sixed from a diner. Café my ass!

I stood for a moment outside the café, looking around. I wasn't quite sure what to do next. It was still quite early, but it had stopped raining and the sun had finally showed itself; it was actually turning into a nice day.

My car was parked in a two-hour zone and I'd been in the restaurant only for... maybe ten minutes, so I stuffed the sandwich into my jacket pocket and took off walking down the street. I needed a quiet place to think, and I figured the Orchard Knob Reservation would be deserted at that time of the morning.

I turned right onto North Orchard Knob Avenue and walked another block to the park entrance. Any other day I might have been more interested in the sights—the park was Ulysses S. Grant's headquarters during the Battle for Chattanooga in 1863. The view from the top of the hill is well worth the walk—that day, however, I was in no mood for sightseeing, or contemplating the momentous events that had taken place there more than a hundred and fifty years ago; I had too much on my mind.

I walked to the top of the hill and sat down on the Illinois monument and was soon lost in thought. Without really thinking about it, I took the sandwich from my pocket and began to peel back the wrapping... and then I saw the note.

Well, well, what do we have here, I thought, *and why am I not surprised?*

I set the sandwich down on the concrete, opened the note, and read: *Starbucks. Hamilton Place. 10 pm.*

What the hell is that about? I thought. *She wants to talk. Why? She doesn't know me... or does she? Maybe it's a setup...* Whatever it was, it didn't matter. I knew right then that I was going to follow up on it.

I folded the note and slipped it into the inside pocket of my jacket, along with Phoebe Marsh's napkin.

I stood up, walked back to the park exit, tossed the uneaten sandwich into a trash can, and walked back to my car and... wouldn't you know it? There was a nasty little surprise waiting for me... well, not so little: Goliath —JoJo, JJ James—was standing beside my car, knife in hand, and all four tires flat.

Aw, come on! I thought; boy was I ever pissed. *Mess with me, but don't mess with my car.*

"Sorry about the tires," the brute said. "The knife just slipped in my hand."

He turned away laughing and started down the street. I wasn't going to let him off that easy. Between the kid and the car, the son of a bitch was going down.

I took off after him at a run, quick enough to surprise him, pulling my gun from its holster just as I reached him.

"Yeah," I growled, "and I'm sorry about your frickin' kneecap. The gun just slipped out of my hand." And I swung the M&P9 as hard as I could—the butt of the gun slammed into the side of his right knee. I heard something crack, and he went down like the sack of garbage that he was.

"Ow, ow, ow," he howled, grabbing the injured knee with both hands. "Freakin' hell... oh ow. You crazy asshole. You just assaulted me. I'm calling the cops." As he fumbled in his pocket, I slammed the butt of the gun into the back of his hand, bringing forth another string of howls and expletives.

"Go ahead, you fat pig." I stood back and looked down at him. "I've got an alibi. I was at the frickin' movies with my friends watching Mary Friggin' Poppins."

I stepped forward again, jammed the barrel of the weapon into his nostrils as he lay there whimpering on the street in front of me.

"Now, JoJo, you're gonna tell me who you work for and why you killed that kid."

"Screw you, asshole."

I slapped his ear with the side of the barrel. He squealed like a stuck pig, and I shoved the gun back into his right nostril.

"Let's try it again. Who do you work for and why did you kill that kid?"

"I don't know what you're talkin' 'bout. I ain't killed nobody."

I smacked him on the ear again and it started to bleed. He wiped his ear with his hand, looked at the blood on his palm, and passed out.

"Some tough guy you are. Can't even stand the sight of your own blood."

I gave him a couple of kicks in the ribs for good measure, then I dialed AAA and asked for a tow truck and how long they'd be. They said they were light on work and that they'd be with me in a couple of minutes.

After ending the call, I stared down at the unconscious goon. He wouldn't be talking anytime soon: he was out cold, but at least I could get a good photo of him and maybe there was a way to find out who he worked for. Thugs like him usually have street cred as well as a rap sheet, and I knew damn well that someone on the street knew who he was. All I had to do was find that someone.

I snapped a picture of his ugly mug with my iPhone, gave him one last kick in the ribs to remember me by, and walked back to the car. Thoroughly pissed off, I leaned on the side, waiting for the tow truck; it arrived just before the goon woke up.

"Hey, is that guy all right?" the tow truck driver asked as he hooked up the car to haul it up onto the flatbed.

"Just another street drunk passed out in the gutter."

"Sheesh, at this time in the morning?"

Goliath stirred, groaned, sat up and looked around, and it was with a certain amount of pleasure that I watched him writhe in pain from what I hoped was a broken rib. The fat bastard could barely breathe. I watched from the cab of the truck as he rolled over and heaved himself up onto to his knees. I rolled down the window.

"Hey, shithead," I shouted. "See you soon."

He glared up at me, bared his teeth, and gave me the finger. I knew right then that I hadn't seen the last of JoJo James.

9

We dropped the car at the tire shop; they were swamped, told me they'd have it done by end of day if I was lucky. I told the guy in charge that wasn't going to work and that there was an extra fifty in it for him if I got the car back by two that afternoon. He told me he'd see what he could do.

I could expect no more than that, so I tipped the truck driver a twenty and he was nice enough to give me a ride home: Ronnie was waiting for me at the door when I got there; it was eleven-forty-five.

Geez, I completely forgot about him.

"Hey, buddy. Sorry, I forgot about you."

"Yeah," he said, dryly. "I noticed. Where's your car?"

"That's a long story. Come on in."

We went inside and I made coffee.

I took a few minutes to fill him in on some of the details of what had happened, then I steered the conversation to the business I had in mind.

"So listen," I said. "I was thinking that maybe, since I'm not working, and kind of at a loose end, I'd start my own business, open a private investigation agency. What d'you think? Finding Phoebe Marsh would be my first case."

"Oh, that's funny." The laughter in his eyes told me he didn't think I was serious.

"Phoebe Marsh?" he said. "Didn't you forget something?

I shook my head and sighed. "What did I forget, Ronnie?"

"Her dad's in jail, probably for the rest of his life, so who's going to pay you?"

"Yeah, well, I don't need money, you know that... and maybe that's why she left her poker money on the table... Hell, Ronnie, I don't care. I don't need a reason. Someone snatched her. I'm going to find her. That's it."

"Wow! You're serious," he said.

"I am. Look, I don't know squat about setting up a new business. So here's the proposition: I'd like you to come on board and handle that kind of stuff for me, set it up... everything. What d'you say?"

He frowned, serious, thoughtful, then said, "You want me to be your business partner? Harry, I don't have that kind of money."

He might not have the money, but I did. My mother was old Chattanooga money, big money. Unfortunately, she died of cancer when I was fifteen, but before she did, she set up a trust for me. I won't tell you how much, but when I turned twenty-five, it was like I won the frickin' lottery... twice. Anyway...

"You don't need any money, Ronnie, and I don't need a partner. I've got all the cash we'll ever need, and then some. I just don't know how to set it all up—the licenses, taxes, accounting, business plan, all that stuff. I'd like you to come work for me, be my business manager. Run the office, maybe get a secretary and some other staff, investigators—"

"I like secretaries."

"I mean for work."

He laughed and stroked his chin as if he had a beard, picked up his coffee, raised the mug in the air, and said, "Why not?"

And we drank to it.

"When do I start? What's the pay? Do I get an office?"

"You start right now. As to your salary... we'll discuss that later, but don't worry, I'll make it worth your while. Do you get an office? Sure, just as soon as *we* get an office. That's your first job, after you register the company... 'Harry Starke Investigations.' I like that."

"Has a nice ring to it. Tell me about what you want for a location."

"The office? I'm thinking somewhere nice, downtown, near the courts and the attorney's offices... That's where it all happens, where the work is. I also thought that maybe you could handle white collar crime investigations..." I smiled. He was going to be very useful. "But first things first. I need some help with this Phoebe Marsh case."

"What kind of help?"

"If what the kid, Stitch, told me before he died is true, that her father sold her, I need to find out who he sold her to. I'm thinking trafficking, human trafficking, sex, prostitution, if so drugs are probably involved as well. All of that means there's an organization behind it; organized crime. I need to find out who, what and where. I think I stumbled into one of their businesses this morning, the Rose Café on East Third, and freaked out a waitress."

"You have a tendency to do that to people. Did you threaten to shoot her?"

"Be serious, Ronnie." I reached into my pocket. "She saw this on the table," I said, laying the napkin in front of him.

"She went into some kind of tailspin and rushed me out of there with a sandwich I didn't order along with a note hidden inside the wrapping paper." I showed him the note.

"You're not going to do this, meet her, are you?" he asked.

"Are you kidding? Of course I am. Absolutely."

"But—"

"But what? It's what I do: investigate, ask questions. Of course I'll meet her. Maybe she has a story to tell. Maybe she knows what happened to Phoebe. Hell, maybe she knows who's running whatever it is that's... Maybe you should come with me."

"You think? Well, maybe I will."

I checked my watch. It was almost two o'clock.

"Yeah, well," I said. "I need to go get my car. You want to take me or do I need to get a taxi?"

He said he would take me.

Ronnie's car was a classic, a beauty—a pristine 1980 Mercedes 280SL. It was his baby and she rode like a dream. Anyway, I had him drop me off at the tire shop and sent him on his way to start working on putting my new business together.

Fortunately, my car was ready and ten minutes later I drove out of the shop on four brand new Michelin Pilot Sports with my wallet seven-hundred-and-fifty big ones lighter, plus the fifty-dollar tip for the speedy turnaround. *Damn! That eight is coming out of Goliath's hide,* I thought, gritting my teeth. But that would have to come later. At that point, all I wanted to do was go home and do some thinking.

10

I parked on the street in front of my condo and exited the car. And, once again I had a creepy feeling that all was not right. I shook it off, mounted the front steps and pointed my key to where the lock used to be... the doorframe around the lock was shattered and the door was slightly ajar.

Ahh, shit! I thought savagely. *Not again.*

Instinctively, I reached for my weapon. Gently, I pushed the door open, took a step back, and waited, listening: nothing.

I took a deep breath and stepped inside. All was quiet, but all was not well: my condo had been trashed.

Stepping around flipped over chairs, trying not to step on scattered papers, picking up slashed sofa cushions, I made my way carefully into the living room and went to the wall safe. I pressed the hidden button on the frame; there was a click and the picture swung open an inch. I opened it the rest of the way and was relieved to find the contents were intact... except for my spare weapon, a twin of the Smith & Wesson 9mm semiautomatic I still held in my hand.

Oh shit! I thought. *That's all I need.*

Whoever it was that had broken into my home was long gone. I went downstairs to the basement, to my office and looked around. *Geez, what a frickin' mess.*

I shoved the gun back into its holster and returned to the kitchen, sorted through the mess, found what I needed, and made some coffee. That done, I went to the living room and flopped down on the couch in front of the big windows; it was starting to rain again. *Damn! Is it ever going to stop?*

I stared out into the mist; the far riverbank was barely visible. I sipped a little coffee, placed the cup down on the side table, and in what seemed only minutes, I was at peace.

I woke a couple of hours later with a crick in my neck and a pain under my arm where the M&P9 was pressing against my bare skin... and it was still raining. I checked my watch: it was almost seven o'clock and I felt like shit. I looked around the room, took in the mess, sighed, rose, and headed for the shower.

Twenty minutes later, and for some reason feeling better than I had in a week, I set about trying to figure out what else my intruders had stolen. Surprise, surprise, nothing seemed to be missing except for my gun, Phoebe's napkin and the note from the sandwich wrapper.

Well, there goes any chance I might have had of

getting prints, I thought. *I should have turned 'em over to Kate yesterday. Well, at least I have photos of them.*

I made more coffee, toasted a bagel, slathered it with cream cheese, and texted Ronnie. I asked him if he'd found us an office and if he had, was it in a secure building?

The next message went to Kate. I told her that my place had been trashed, that I was okay, but the napkin and wrapper were missing. I figured it would be a good idea to keep her in the loop.

I took my coffee and bagel to my office, shook my head at the mess, then fired up my laptop, found the number for a local security company and made a note of it. No way was this going to happen again.

I sat for a minute, trying to get my head around the mess I'd gotten myself into. I couldn't; none of it made any sense. I shook my head, changed gears, and thought again about Goliath.

JoJo? Meh, I don't think so. Goliath suits me just fine, I thought, as the image of his exploding face when I sank my fist into his gut flashed through my mind, and I couldn't help but smile.

I called Kate.

"Hey, Velda," I said when she answered. "Have you got a minute? I have some questions."

I heard her laugh.

"Sure," she said, "but first tell me what happened at the condo. Are you okay?"

"Oh yeah, I'm fine, but the place is trashed and... they took my spare M&P9, along with Phoebe's note and the one from the café. They were both on my desk."

"Geez, Harry. That's not good, your weapon. You'll need to file a report... No, I'll file it right now. If it's used to commit a crime, you need to be covered. Give me the serial number."

I read it off to her, then said, "Kate, I've got to get to the bottom of this, and I have almost nothing to go on. I have a meeting tonight with the waitress who handed me the note. Maybe she has some answers. Other than that, there's just the big guy, Joseph James, JoJo. What do you have on him?"

"He's a nobody, Harry. He has a rap sheet a mile long, but it's all for petty crime, and he's been arrested several times for assault and extortion. Seems he works as muscle for anyone willing to pay him. Here's the thing, though: it's all old stuff. He's been clean for almost three years. Either he's turned the page and is going straight, which we know he hasn't, or someone is looking after him."

"Yeah," I said. "That's what I figured, but who? He's an animal, and high profile. He'd be more trouble than he's worth."

"I don't know, Harry. Tell me about this meeting... You want me to come along with you?"

"No, but thanks for the offer. If she knows anything, I need her to talk, and—"

She interrupted me, "And I don't like your methods, right?"

I smiled; she knew me better than I knew myself.

"Oh, come on, Kate. When did I ever put the screws to a woman?"

"Never, that I know of, but there's always a first time. And you're out on your own now, no oversight, no one to answer to, except me, if you break the law."

"Me, break the law? Never. Okay, I gotta go. See you later?"

"Maybe. Just be careful, Harry." She disconnected.

A basic Google search for James' name turned up nothing, which told me that whoever he was working for knew what they were doing. I sat for a long moment, staring at the screen, willing it to tell me something, anything, but it remained silent. I sighed.

I was pretty good at tracking people, but if I was going to make this PI thing work, I figured I'd need someone a whole lot better than me, and I thought I knew exactly who that someone was.

I tapped the keyboard, found what I was looking for, closed the laptop, grabbed my coat and weapon, and headed out the door. It was almost eight.

Five minutes later, I was on my way to the only twenty-four-seven Internet cafe in town. Yeah, it was Friday evening and the place would undoubtedly be busy, but that didn't matter. I knew they'd be there—they always were—the hardcore computer geeks with their glazed eyes, sallow skin, and brains that thought only in binary code. With any luck, the guy I had in mind would be one of them.

The streets were quiet, which was good after the hustle of the past few days. It seemed like things had been going nonstop since I picked up the kid, Phoebe Marsh, in the rainstorm. The quiet solitude as I drove through the rain gave me a chance to think.

Why Phoebe? Did her old man really sell her? Maybe he did. They sure as hell went to a lot of trouble to grab her that night. I guess it could be they had an investment in her... if he didn't, there had to be another reason, but what?

And who the hell is this Goliath guy working for and why did he slash my frickin' tires? It couldn't have been just for the hell of it... Maybe they were trying to keep me there at the Rose Café. Hmm... And what about that Penelope? Will she really turn up at Starbucks, or was she part of a trap... to set me up? Oh yeah, whether she turns up tonight or not, I need to talk to her again.

The blue light of the sign appeared on my left, snapping me out of my thoughts. I made a U-turn and parked in front of the Blue Tornado. *Who the hell thought that one up, I wonder?*

I remembered the place from a couple of years ago when it had been a sleazy bar cum whorehouse. The city had shut them down, not because it was a health hazard, which it was, but because two people had died right there, out front, during a couple of drive-by shootings.

The heavy wooden door with a peephole in situ still smelled a little of cigarettes and booze.

I pushed the door open and stepped inside, and again the twin stale smells assailed my olfactory system: ugh. It was dark inside and must have been about as close to heaven as a geek could expect to get: dim blue lighting and little else but the glow from a dozen or so computer screens. It wasn't as busy as I'd expected; just five customers, all of them under eighteen, I guessed. Fortunately, one of them was the kid I was looking for. I'd gotten a break at last.

"Hey, kid. You got a minute?"

Tim Clarke, the kid from the poker game at the Sorbonne, just about leaped out of his skin. He jumped up from his seat and threw his body in front of the computer screen.

The kid's up to no good.

"Whattt?" he stuttered, wide-eyed, terrified.

"Hey, it's okay. Calm down. We met at the poker game at the Sorbonne, remember?"

"Um... yeah... sure," he said with his back still to the screen. He was pretty nervous which told me he was either surfing porn or hacking, and I was betting on hacking. Either way, he was just what I needed.

"I need a minute. Is that okay?"

He nodded but didn't move away from the screen.

"You remember the girl that was playing with us that night?"

Again, he nodded.

"Someone grabbed her. Threw her into the back of a van right after she got up from the table. She was abducted. I'm trying to find her."

"I don't know anything about that. I swear."

"No, no, kid. I know that. Look, I'm a private investigator and I..." Hell, I knew basically what I wanted, but I was new to the game and had no idea how to tell him.

"Okay, look," I said, sitting down on his chair. "I've

got leads, but I need help fleshing 'em out. I need someone with your kind of skills. You interested in a job? I pay well."

The surprised look on his face was just short of amusing. He poked at the bridge of his glasses with an extraordinarily long forefinger, and frowned, like he was thinking about it.

"Doing what?" he asked.

"Computer stuff. Geeky stuff. IT. Finding people, tracing phone numbers, anything computer related, maybe even a little hacking. You up for it?"

He scratched his head and pushed up his glasses. "I... I don't know."

"Let me guess," I said. "You're what... sixteen, seventeen... still live with your mom. You come here because you have no privacy at home, on your mom's computer. You're probably surfing porn or hacking something on this one, right?" The minute I said hacking, his eyes got wide. *Oh yes! He's frickin' perfect.*

"Seventeen... I'm seventeen. But... I... um..." He was scared. Probably thought I was gonna turn him in.

"Come on, kid. You can do better than this. Who are you hacking? A bank? The government? Somebody else's government? All hackers get caught sooner or later, and they end up in jail. You don't want that, now do you?"

He shook his head.

"So come work for me and use your talent legally. I'll pay you well, and you can pick out whatever equipment you think you need. You can have your own machine... top-of-the-line stuff, and your own place? And I'm not talking about sharing a prison cell with a roommate named Dragon." *That got him.*

He stepped away from the screen, grabbed a chair, sat down, and poked his glasses again. I looked at the screen.

"Shit! You're hacking the IRS? Oh man, as much as the bastards have hounded me in the past and how I'd love for you to completely wipe my records, it's wrong and you shouldn't be doing it for anyone else either."

He looked at me with puppy dog eyes, tears welling up in them.

"You're not going to tell my mom, are you?"

Geez. The kid doesn't care about jail, all he's worried about is his mom.

"No. I won't tell her if you promise to knock it off and come work for me. I'll give you an office. You get to set up the network, buy all the computers and any other tech toys you think you might need. What do you say?"

He turned back to the computer and with a few keystrokes he was out of the IRS database, clicked the mouse, and shut down the computer. He pushed back the chair, stood up, grabbed his backpack, looked at me and said, "When do I start?"

11

I gave the kid my phone number and told him to call me on Monday morning. I also made him promise to go straight home and not hack anything else. He did as he was asked, and I believed him. He seemed like a smart kid, just a little misdirected. *I can fix that.*

I left him to it and headed out toward Hamilton Place and my meeting with Penelope. Ten o'clock, she'd said in her note, but I had no idea what I might be walking into so I intended to get there early.

I ordered a Tall dark roast, found a seat in the corner by the front window with a good view of both Hamilton Place Boulevard and Bams Drive, and settled down to wait. If she came, I'd see her coming and I'd see her park.

As it happened, I didn't have long to wait. I had no idea what she was driving, but when I saw a black VW Touareg drive slowly onto the lot from Bams Drive, I had a certain feeling that it was her. I watched as she parked the VW and exited the car... and then, for just a moment, my view of her was obscured as a car passed slowly between her and the building. It slowed for a second then gained speed, squealing its tires as it sped out onto Hamilton Place Boulevard and away toward Shallowford Road.

I watched it go then stood and turned toward the door to meet her. As I did, I glanced out of the window and saw her lying on the asphalt beside her car, blood pooling around her head.

I rushed out of the door and knelt down beside her. Her eyes were wide open, her throat pulsing, gulping, pumping blood from the small gunshot wound to her neck and another in her upper left shoulder.

She was dying, and there wasn't a damn thing I could do about it. I did what I could. I grabbed her neck between fingers and thumb, my thumb on the bullet wound, trying to stop the flow.

I looked desperately around. The front window of Starbucks was crowded with faces. I waved at the window, making signals for someone to phone for an ambulance, and held on to her, talking to her, telling her she was doing fine, that she was going to be okay, knowing damn well that she wasn't. I knew it for sure and I'm rarely wrong.

I don't know how long it was before the ambulance arrived. I know it seemed like hours, but it was probably less than ten minutes. Anyway, whatever, she was still alive when the paramedics took over from me.

I remember a female paramedic grabbing my wrist and pulling me away, and I remember I fell back on my ass and scrambled back out of the way.

I stood and watched as they staunched the bleeding

and then loaded her into the ambulance. It was then I realized I still had no idea, other than her first name, Penelope, who she was. I ran to my car, scrambled in behind the wheel, hit the starter and followed the ambulance out onto Shallowford Road and all the way to Erlanger Emergency Center.

I grabbed my iPhone and called Kate.

"Oh shit," she said. "Thank God, it's you. I heard the call on the radio, and I knew when I heard Starbucks that it must be you. I'm on my way to Erlanger. Where are you? What happened? Are you okay?"

"It's okay, Velda. Someone shot Penelope. They got to her in the parking lot. I saw it happen... well, not exactly, but near enough. I'll explain later. I'll see you at the hospital, okay?"

"Yes, okay, but please... stop with the Velda. It's no longer funny."

PENELOPE ROSS DIED *in the emergency room at Erlanger at ten after eleven that same evening. Cause of death was one of two .22 long-rifle bullets that entered her neck at the left side slicing through the carotid artery, the spinal column between C_4 and C_5, severing the spinal cord.*

"That's two," I said, despondently. "Two innocent people dead in two days and all because of me."

"Death does seem to follow you around, Harry," Kate said gloomily. "Obviously, someone didn't want her talking to you, but who?"

We were seated together, side by side, in the waiting room. I shook my head. I was as baffled as she was.

"No one knew I was meeting her."

"Don't be stupid, Harry!" The voice was male, and it was right behind me. I swiveled on my chair, my hand instinctively going for my weapon.

"Chief," I said, standing up and turning to face him. "You shouldn't creep up on people like that, but why am I not surprised to see you here?"

The man was a bear, taller than me by an inch, and I hated it. Now you know why I never sit with my back to a door, only that time I did. My bad!

"Sit down, Harry, and talk to me. What the hell have you gotten yourself into?"

I said that Chief Wesley Johnston is a bear, and he is. He's big, brash, a martinet and, to most of the Chattanooga Police Department, intimidating, but not to me. I'd lost count of the run-ins I'd had with the SOB. He was a hands-on administrator, micromanaged his senior staff, and came down hard on those who were unfortunate enough to get on his wrong side. I was one of those. Between him and his version of Igor, Henry Finkle, my ten years on the force had not been... shall we say, easy?

The chief maintained that I wasn't a team player, which wasn't true. Kate and I had been one hell of a great team. Our closing rate was second to none. To Johnston, "team player" meant that you did as you were told, always and without question. So in that respect, he was right: I wasn't a team player.

I was in no mood for him that evening, but him being

who he was, I had no choice but to tell him everything... well, almost everything.

He listened without interrupting until I'd finished, then he sat back in his chair, placed his elbows on its arms and steepled his fingers together at his lips and blew gently on them, staring over them at me as he did so.

"You've been gone barely two months," he said, finally, "and you've gotten yourself involved in two murders and a kidnapping. What the hell is it with you, Harry?"

"With me? Not a damn thing. This all began with a simple game of poker. Do you really think—"

"No, I don't," he interrupted me. "I think it's about the money. It's always about the money. Marsh screwed the wrong people. They want their money. It's that simple... No, it's not simple at all. What is simple is that you're no longer a police officer and I want you to stay the hell out of it. You understand?"

"Who's got the case, Wesley?"

I thought he was going to explode at my use of his first name, but he was right. I wasn't a cop anymore and didn't need to use his title... and anyway, screw him.

"Lieutenant Cable, not that it's any business of yours. I mean it, Harry; stay out of it."

"No can do, Wes. I'm a private investigator now, and I intend to get the bastard that killed the kid and Penelope Ross, and the piece o' crap that paid him to do it. And yeah, I know who did it. I saw him kill the kid right in front of me for God's sake. My word not enough for you?"

"You're... a PI?" He was dumbfounded. "When the hell did that happen? No matter, I don't want to know.

Nothing's changed. You stay the hell out of it or I'll have Cable throw you in the can... James had a cast iron alibi; your word against his and a dozen of his friends. He couldn't have done it, no matter what you saw. That's what his lawyer will say."

"Oh, come on, Chief. You know better than that. Hell, arrest the piece of shit and let's find out who his lawyer is... Look, I'll collaborate with Eric Cable, but I'm going to do what I have to do. You know I will, so why don't you just let me get on with it and leave me alone?"

He stared at me, then at Kate, then at me again, hesitated, then said, "I'll let Cable know, but it's his decision... PI my ass." And with that, he got up and strode away.

"Well," Kate said, with a smile, "that went well."

Even though I was in no mood to, I grinned at her, then said, "Better than I thought it would." I checked my watch. "It's late. We need to go. You have to work in the morning and I have to... Geez, I have no idea what. Why don't you go on home? I'll talk to you tomorrow." And she did.

12

I'd planned to spend the following day, Friday, catching up on a whole bunch of stuff that I was supposed to have completed weeks ago: I figured if I was going to open a business, I'd better get my life in order.

It was well after midnight when I left the hospital. I was exhausted; the effects of the past couple of days were beginning to catch up with me, so I decided I'd go home, drink a little Laphroaig, eat a sandwich, relax, and then go to bed, and that's what I did... sort of.

When I arrived back to the condo, there was an unmarked cruiser parked on the road outside.

Kate? I thought, smiling.

I found her in the living room, trying to tidy the place, picking up stuff and putting it away. Oh, yeah, I meant to do it myself earlier, but... well, you know how it is.

"What are you doing here?" I asked, throwing my jacket and holster onto a stool by the breakfast bar in the kitchen. "I thought you were going home?"

"You looked like you needed a friend," she said. "As to what am I doing, what does it look like?" She held up a magazine. "Do you know you have magazines from the nineties?"

"Yeah, I'm saving them for the articles. Kate, you didn't have to come over. I was going to clean up in the morning."

She tossed the magazine onto the bookshelf, picked up a couch pillow and started fluffing it.

"Boy, did you ever piss somebody off?" she said, throwing the pillow onto the couch. "They slash your tires and now this. They must be into some really bad stuff to work this hard to discourage you. I hope you get 'em... 'cause Detective Lieutenant Eric Cable couldn't find his own ass with the light on."

She came over, slipped her arms around my neck and kissed me lightly on the lips. "But not tonight, sweet prince. Tonight Velda needs Mikey, so come on." She took my hand and led me to the bedroom.

We had only taken a few steps when I pulled her close and kissed her properly. She kissed me back, then pushed me away, grabbed my hand with both of hers and, tugging hard, she backed into the bedroom.

"Aw, crap!" I said. The sheets had been slashed and the bed was a mess.

She looked at me, smiling, and laughed. "Ooo, brutal. Those were your favorite sheets."

"Bastards!" I snarled, and then stormed off down the hall and fetched another set of sheets from the linen closet. By the time I returned, Kate had the bed stripped and ready for the new sheets.

"You can always use them for cleaning, something you don't do often enough. Maybe they were trying to tell you something."

"Yeah, yeah. And maybe one of these days I'll get a maid."

"Oui, Oui monsieur. Maybe a French one," she said in a poor French accent. "I can wear one of those leettle black and white outfits, the ones with the ruffles."

"Hah," I said. "They don't make 'em to fit busty girls like you. You'd be sticking out of it... Okay then. We'll go shopping tomorrow.

"You think?" she asked and threw a pillow at my head.

I was glad she had a sense of humor because I was still fuming; those sheets had cost me a bundle.

She took the sheets from me and shook out the one with the corner pockets.

"Grab the other side," she said as she tucked the fitted sheet around the corners of the mattress.

I did, and the next thing I knew, the top sheet was covering my head and she was laughing as she jumped into the middle of the bed and landed on her knees.

Geez, she's beautiful, I thought as I grabbed the covers and threw them in a pile on the end of the bed. She sat on her haunches, slipped the Glock and holster off her belt, set it on the nightstand, pointed her finger at me and motioned for me to join her. And I did. Who the hell cared about making the rest of the bed? It was going to get messed up anyway... And it did.

13

It was seven o'clock when I woke to sunshine beaming in through the window directly in my face that Friday morning. Kate was already up, showered and gone to work, but her scent still lingered on the fresh sheets and in the bathroom. Anyway, there was coffee in the pot and a note to say she'd call me later.

I took a leisurely shower, poured a mug of coffee, took it out onto the patio and, wearing only a towel, sat quietly, contemplating the events of the past several days. By eight thirty, I was back inside with a second cup of coffee and an egg sandwich. I was kind of getting used to the lazy life, and liking it too but, as they say, all good things...

I placed the empty mug and plate in the sink and went back to the bedroom and dressed.

It was a little after nine-thirty when Ronnie called.

"Hey there, Sleeping Beauty," I said, brightly. "How was your evening?"

"Nothing special, except that someone stole my car. How about you?"

"How the hell did that happen?" I asked. "Oh, I know, you left the top down again, didn't you?"

He didn't answer, which told me that he did. I sighed, shook my head, then filled him in on the events of the previous evening, including my run-in with Chief Johnston at the hospital.

"Nice," he said. Ronnie always was one for the understatement. "How are you feeling?"

"Nice," I said, mimicking him. "Kate stayed over. How much better can it get?"

"Not much," he said. "Hey, I've found us an office, a couple of blocks from the Flatiron Building on Georgia Avenue. It's the perfect location, close to the courthouse and bail bonds."

"Sounds about right," I said. "How big?"

"Big enough for you, me, a cute secretary and room to grow."

"Talk like that in front of Kelly and she'll cut your—"

Kelly was, is, Ronnie's wife. A flirt he might be, but Kelly was the love of his life.

"Send me the address," I said, "and I'll meet you there in an hour. I'm on my way over to Doc McDowell. It's time for my wellness exam. Shouldn't take long. You have a ride, right?"

"Yes, I have a ride. I'll use Kelly's Subaru. See you in an hour, boss."

"Oh, come on. Let's not start that... Hey, remember

that kid from the Sorbonne you beat at poker the other night?"

"Which one? There were two."

"Tim Clarke. I hired him last night to do our tech stuff."

"Geez, Harry, that kid can't be more than fifteen."

"Seventeen, but he's a hacker with some mean computer skills. We can use him. I asked him to call me this morning. I'll have him meet us there and you get him set up, okay?"

"Whatever you say, *boss*." The sarcastic tone was a bit much.

"Don't do that, Ronnie. I'd hate to have to fire you even before you start work."

"Hey, I have started. You already owe me."

"Later, Ronnie. Don't forget to send me that address."

I disconnected, feeling pretty good about the way things were shaping up. My new business would soon be a reality, but my first case as a PI was not going quite so well. There were a lot of big pieces of the puzzle missing, the biggest being Phoebe.

Where the hell is she? I thought. *Her father sold her? He can't do that, she's an adult... At least she said she is... Damn it, Harry, he couldn't do it anyway; she's a human being, for God's sake. Geez, I hope she's still alive and if she is, I hope to hell they haven't completely brainwashed her...*

DANIEL McDOWELL WAS my regular provider, my GP, and an old friend. I went to him because I knew he was discreet. I'd known him since I was in high school at McCallie. He had a small practice over off Gunbarrel Road along with about fifty other doctors in the medical neighborhood. He'd also helped me out on a case with the CPD a couple of years back and played golf with my father every once in a while, and with me not so often.

More giant leprechaun than man, his large belly would shake like a 1926 Model-T driving through a field of potholes whenever he laughed... and he laughed a lot: a big, happy-go-lucky Irishman with wispy white hair, a crooked smile, and an infectious laugh—always laughing at his own jokes whether they were funny or not. The Doc had a great mind and an eye for detail along with a sincere love of mankind. How he did it—like everyone— was beyond me. There are a lot of people in this world who don't even deserve to live, let alone be liked, Goliath being one of them. But the Doc would like even him, I'm sure.

The little bell jingled as I opened the door to his office. It was still early, but the Doc didn't really have set hours. He operated his practice almost like a walk-in clinic, which it wasn't, but he never turned anyone away. He firmly believed that ailments wouldn't wait, so why should the patient. He's one of a kind, and I wished there were more like him.

I checked in with Mandy, his receptionist/daughter, and took a seat next to a striking young girl in a tight skirt with long legs crossed at the knee and an iPhone at her ear. She was gorgeous. I tagged her to be about twenty, twenty-one, five nine with coffee and cream skin, a full head of bushy black hair, and a smile that could melt a heart. It sounded like she was talking to her mom or dad, or maybe both, laughing and joking about a girl at school she'd been dating. There was something special about her, an intelligent air that was uncommon in girls her age... and the accent... West Indian? Fabulous!

Mandy opened the glass sliding window. "Jacque. There was a problem with your card. Do you have another one?"

"Momma, I gotta go. Love to you and Dad."

She stood and went to the window. "Prob-lem? What prob-lem?"

"They declined your card; I'm sorry."

She rubbed her forehead and pulled on her hair. "It must have been dat payment for school. Can you hold off for a week or two? I lost my job, and I'm looking for another one. I'm sure something will come along soon."

"How about I hire you?" I said. "I'll give you an advance so you can pay your bill." *Where the hell did that come from, Harry?* I thought.

She looked me up and down and gave a little scoff. "You're kidding, right? That's the worst pick-up line I ever did hear. Forget it. I'm not that kind of girl."

I grinned at her and said, "No, seriously. I'm a private investigator and I'm looking to hire a personal assistant. Tell her I'm okay, Mandy."

"He's the best of the best, Jacque. If you don't take the job, I will." At that I had to smile: Mandy would never have left her dad, but I appreciated the vote of confidence.

"A PI? You must be a good one. How else would you know to hire someone with a Bachelor's in Criminology without interviewing them?"

"Like Mandy said, I'm the best of the best. How much is her bill?"

Jacque held up her hand. "Not so fast. What's your name?"

"Harry Starke. And you're Jacque." I watched as she raised her eyebrows. "I heard Mandy call your name."

Her smile lit up the room and her laugh could brighten anyone's day. Her hand went down and reached out for me to shake it.

"Jacque Hale, personal assistant to Harry Starke, private investigator. When do I start? Oh wait, my schedule is kind of hectic right now. I haven't graduated yet, but I'll be done in a few months, but I can start this afternoon, say at one o'clock. Is that okay?"

I took her hand and shook it. "Perfect." In my jacket pocket was an old card from a guy selling life insurance. I turned it over and wrote my phone number on the back.

"Now, if you'll give me yours, I'll have Ronnie text you the address."

She nodded and held out her hand. I looked at it then at her. She was smiling... then I got it.

"Oh, okay," I said and handed my iPhone to her.

She entered the number and handed it back to me.

"One o'clock then, boss?"

"Don't call me that. My name's Harry. Okay?"

I took out my wallet and handed a credit card to Mandy. "Pay her bill and send me a receipt."

Sometimes things just happen for a reason. I could tell Jacque was holding back the urge to hug me and that was okay. She'd have plenty of opportunities to do so down the road. In the meantime...

Doc McDowell came out of the office door, walked straight up to Jacque and gave her a big hug. "It's negative. You're not pregnant." His belly went up and down as he laughed.

"That's a relief. I can't wait to tell my girlfriend." The baffled look on my face must have said it all. "It's a joke," she said, laughing. "He says it to me every time I come in. I'm gay. Can't get pregnant from a girl. Get it?"

It doesn't happen often, but I blushed which made all three of them laugh.

"Well, it looks like the great Harry Starke has met his match," Dan said, his great stomach shaking.

"Good thing because I just hired her."

"Two of my favorite people working together side by side. Oh, the fun you'll have. Come on back, Jacque."

"You better let my new boss go first. He's a busy man, and I wouldn't want to get fired before I even start."

I was in kind of a hurry. "You sure?" I asked her.

"Absolutely."

She was going to work out just fine.

We went back into the examining room and shut the door. He had his nurse pull three vials of blood and as she laid each one down, I couldn't help but think about that thug Goliath, and I had to smile.

"Do you want to share your little joke with the rest of us, Harry?"

"Ha, nothing really. I was just thinking about a killer I know who faints at the sight of his own blood. Big guy too, about six-seven and three hundred pounds of fat."

"Well, if his cholesterol doesn't kill him, the diabetes will," he said as he watched his nurse put a cotton ball on my arm and pull out the needle.

He turned to a cabinet and grabbed a specimen cup, scrawled my name on the side and handed it to me. "Put your sample in this and leave it on the sink."

I went into the bathroom, did as he asked, opened the door, and bumped into Jacque. *Oh great, my pee's still in there.*

"Pardon me," she said. "I didn't know you were in there." She squeezed by me, shut the door, and a second later I heard a hoot of laughter. The door opened again and a beaming Jacque handed me the container.

"Well boss, looks like our first meeting has been christened." And she shut the door still laughing. That was twice in less than thirty minutes she'd made me blush. This was going to be one hell of a working relationship.

"I'll take that," Mandy said as she reached around me.

McDowell was standing in the doorway of the examining room doing his best not to laugh, but it didn't work.

"I can't wait to see what she does to you in an office,"

he said, holding his stomach. "You're good to go, Harry. I'll let you know the results as soon as I have them."

"Thanks," I said, feeling a little humiliated.

"Bye, boss," came a yell from inside the bathroom.

"See ya," I yelled back and left with the two of them still laughing at me.

Geez.

14

It was about a half hour drive to the new office and I was running a bit behind, but I wasn't too bothered. Ronnie would wait; what else could he do?

The last several days had been a whirlwind in so many ways, but having managed to gather together a crew in such a short time, be it still very much an unknown quantity, was pretty miraculous. In fact, if I didn't know better, I'd say it was meant to be.

I pulled the car door shut just as my phone rang; it was the kid.

"Hi... um, Mr. Starke. It's Tim Clarke. You hired me... on Friday. You told me to call you this morning, remember?"

"That I do, kid. Do you have a car?"

"I can borrow my mom's."

"Never mind. Give me your address and I'll pick you up. Can you text it to me?"

"Sure."

My phone beeped. *That was fast.* I put the address into the Garmin on the dash.

"I'll be there in fifteen minutes. Can you be ready?"

"Yes, sir. I'll be ready."

"Okay."

What a difference between this kid and Jacque. Maybe I can help him to get a little confidence.

The kid lived in East Ridge on Wynnwood Road. I was still on Gunbarrel so it wouldn't be too much of a detour, but the traffic was heavy and I was going to be really late.

"Call Ronnie," I said.

"Calling Ronnie Hall cell phone."

The phone rang four times before he answered. "Hey, sorry," he said. "I just got finished signing the lease. There was another guy here wanting the space so I had to act. I hope that's okay."

"Works for me," I said. "Listen, I have to swing by and pick up the geek. I've also hired a secretary. She said she'd start this afternoon."

"Fantastic! Is she lovely?"

I smiled. "Gorgeous, but I don't think she's your type."

"If she's gorgeous, she's my type. What's your ETA?"

"Traffic's a little heavy... say thirty minutes."

Ronnie sighed audibly. "I need coffee, Harry. Meet me at Starbucks?"

"No... Yes, okay. Let's do the one on Brainerd Road,

but on your way, stop off somewhere and buy a coffee maker, and some Dark Italian Roast and all the fixin's."

"You got it, boss. Call me when you get close." He hung up.

15

The kid's house was on a corner in a nice middle-class neighborhood. It was a red brick affair with white trim, a big porch with white rails, and a large grassy yard. No one would ever suspect that a genius hacker lurked in this basement.

I'd barely put the car into park when the kid came hurrying out of the front door, backpack slung over his shoulder and yelling back into the house.

"Bye, Mom. I love you," he shouted over his shoulder.

His mom came to the door and looked out after him, waving. By the look of her, I guessed she was a single mom in her early forties, a little plain and tired, mousy brown hair swept back into a ponytail, and she was wearing an apron like she was doing some baking.

I bet she has to work two jobs to pay for the house and keep food on the table, I thought. *Maybe the geek'll be able to help her out, now that he has a real job.*

He hopped into the car, put his backpack on the floor,

and strapped in. The scared and awkward kid of a couple of days ago had disappeared—*for how long*, I wondered—and all that was left was an excited youngster with a bright spark of enthusiasm.

"Relax kid. We got plenty of time." It suddenly dawned on me that it was Monday. "Don't you have school today?"

"No. I graduated two years ago."

"You graduated from high school at fifteen? Holy crap!" *The kid really was a genius.*

The shy, awkward kid came back as he wiped the sweat from his upper lip with his sleeve. "It was... nothing. Um... I just got easy teachers. I'm afraid I dropped out of college, though, last year."

I didn't wanna make him feel any more awkward than I already had so I changed the subject.

"You drink coffee?"

His eyes lit up. "I love coffee. Anything with caffeine."

"Good. We're meeting my business manager at Starbucks. I'll buy you one and you two can chat about your job. You've already met him. He's the guy that beat you at poker at the Sorbonne. His name is Ronnie Hall."

He looked at me almost scared.

"It's okay," I said. "He's a good guy. You can learn a lot from each other. But no poker during office hours, got it?"

He nodded. "What are we going to be working on?" he asked.

"A couple of things. First, I need you to get set up. Go

buy whatever you need. Ronnie will pay for it. When that's done and you're up and running, I'm going to need you to dig into... well, there's a guy I want you to track down, and... we'll talk about it later. That okay?"

He laughed, shoved his glasses up the bridge of his nose and said, "Oh yeah. I can find anyone or anything, but most of what I need I'll have to order. I'll need a laptop right away, but I can get that, and a few other easy items at Best Buy."

"Good. Whatever you need is okay with me. I'll give you everything I have when we get to the office."

We pulled up outside Starbucks; Ronnie was already standing outside with a cup in his hand. I let the kid out and went hunting for a parking space.

This time of day on a Monday morning—partway between breakfast and lunchtime—it was murder trying to find a spot. After circling the place once but finding nothing, I drove out onto the street and circled the block. I found an empty spot at the China Moon restaurant. It wasn't yet open so I was able to park the Maxima there. I walked the bock and a half back to Starbucks and found the kid standing by himself, looking awkward and out of place.

"Where's Ronnie?" I asked.

"The police took him."

"*What the heck?* When? Why?"

"Just now. They said something about murder. They wanted to talk to you too."

They must have some information about Stitch, or Penelope.

"Come on, kid. We're going to the police department. You'll be able to learn a lot through this process. I wonder why they didn't just wait for me? Did Ronnie follow them with the car?"

The kid looked puzzled. "Um, he would have had a hard time driving with his hands cuffed."

"Cuffed? They arrested him?"

"Yeah."

"There's something wrong here. Let's go." I grabbed the kid by the backpack and steered him back down the street to where I'd parked my car.

"I... um... should probably go home now," he said. "I can take the bus."

"Look kid, I didn't kill anybody—well, not this time— and neither did Ronnie. Something's going on and I need you to help me figure it out." I stopped and looked him square in the eyes. "You have to trust me. I won't let anything happen to you." When I said that, deja vu brought me back to the night with Phoebe.

Not going to happen again, I thought, grimly.

16

We were back in the car and already on Amnicola and heading toward the police department when I called Kate.

"Kate! What the hell's going on. They've just arrested Ronnie for murder, at least that's what I'm told."

"I don't know what you're talking about. Wait. They just walked through the door. I'll call you right back."

She hung up before I could tell her we were on our way. I parked out front and barreled straight in through the front doors, waving to the admin at the desk to buzz me in. Fortunately, she knew me; the security door opened and I charged on in with the kid in tow.

I went straight to Kate's office. Ronnie was in there with Kate and the king of blubber, Sergeant Lonnie Guest. Back then, there was no love lost between Lonnie and me. We'd known each other since the police academy, and for some reason the fat bastard hated my guts. I didn't think too highly of him either, but there you go.

"You're under arrest, Starke, for the murder of Benny Brown," Lonnie said, up in my face, handcuffs out, grabbing at my arms, trying to cuff me.

"Get your hands off me, Lonnie, before I beat the crap out of you."

"Great!" he snarled. "You just added threatening a police officer to those charges."

Kate interrupted. "Back off, Lonnie; go get us some coffee. I'll handle this. Come on in, Harry."

"Black," I said with a smirk. He looked furious as he waddled off towards the coffee machine.

I followed Kate into the office and closed the door. "What the hell is going on?" I asked as she uncuffed Ronnie.

"I was hoping you could tell me. They found Ronnie's Mercedes."

She sat down behind her desk, waved a hand for me to sit too. I did, so did Ronnie. There were no more chairs so Tim stood behind me.

"Oh yeah? They found it. That's good, right? So why did Lonnie arrest him, and what's it got to do with me?"

"The car was in the river—well, half in and half out. Someone drove it off the parking lot off Dixie Drive, back of the Champion's Tennis Club. Benny Brown was in the trunk, dead, shot in the head."

"Oh," I said.

"Yeah oh!" she said dryly. "A dead body in Ronnie's car... And possibly the murder weapon in the trunk with the body, a Smith and Wesson M&P9... Henry Finkle is salivating at the thought of locking you up, Harry."

"Who the hell is Benny Brown?" Ronnie asked.

"He is—was—a nasty little rat," Kate said. "An ex-con, dealt drugs, guns, girls, whatever. He worked for Shady Tree."

Why does that name keep coming up whenever someone shows up dead?

Kate looked over my shoulder at the kid who was quivering behind me. She looked up at me.

"Who's he?"

"He's my tech guy. Tim Clarke meet Kate Gazarra."

"My pleasure," she said. "What's he doing here?"

"Well, we were just meeting up with Ronnie to go to our new office when your fat friend, Lonnie Guest, arrested him—"

Kate interrupted me, "What the hell's with you, Harry? You two think this is all a joke? Lonnie has probable cause; he thinks the gun puts you at the crime scene. This is serious. Lonnie wants to hold you for murder."

"Aw, come on, Kate. It all circumstantial, you know that. You took the missing weapon report yourself, and you know what happened at my place; someone trashed it. You saw it yourself, *remember*? It's obvious: they took the gun and the notes, stole Ronnie's car, and planted the gun with the body. We didn't have anything to do with killing this guy."

Kate stood up, pulled her hair back into a ponytail and walked to the window. "I know it and you know it, but nobody else does, and circumstantial works both ways." She turned again to face us, her expression serious.

"I... I think they're telling the truth," a small voice said.

We all looked at Tim, and he looked at the ground. *The kid had more of a spine then I gave him credit for.*

Kate walked over, put her hand on his shoulder and smiled that million-dollar smile. "I'm listening. Why do you think they're telling the truth?"

Tim looked at me and licked his lips. They were dry from mouth breathing through all the excitement. "You were a cop, right?" I nodded. "So you know stuff; you know what goes on, right? So why would you guys leave a body and your gun in your own car where it was sure to be found: the back of the Champion's Tennis Club? It makes no sense."

We all knew that, with maybe the exception of Ronnie, but I was impressed that the kid had figured it out.

"You have an expert here," Kate said and smiled.

"Indeed I do," I said. "You just earned your first paycheck, Tim." I patted him on the back. "Damn, I must have really pissed someone off for them to go to all this trouble." I paused, thought for a minute, then continued, "I need to find out who's behind—"

"No," Kate said firmly. "You'll stay out of it. It's a homicide case. I'll turn it over to Cable and let him handle it from here. You got that, Harry?"

I grinned at her and said, "I think I'll start by talking to Lester Tree."

"Oh, hell," she said, shaking her head, exasperated. "You make my life a misery."

"Oh, stop worrying. I know what I'm doing. Ronnie, you and Tim go and get started setting up the office. Buy him a computer, desks, whatever you need. You also need to take care of my new PA. Her name's Jacque Hale. She'll be there at one... You did text her the address, right?"

"Come on, Harry," Ronnie said. "You know better than to ask a question like that; of course I did."

"Good," I said. "Kate, we're out of here. We have work to do. I'll call you later."

"Stay out of trouble, Harry."

I opened the door and ran right into Lonnie. The coffee slopped down the front of his uniform.

"Damn it, Starke," he yelled. "Where do you think you're going?"

"Out for a burger. I'd invite you, but I can see you've already had one too many."

I pushed past him, followed by Tim and Ronnie. I could feel Lonnie's eyes burning a hole in the back of my head as he raged at Kate for letting us go.

She is one patient lady, I thought, smiling to myself.

17

Finding Shady wouldn't be hard. He was predictable, always hung out at the same place on Bailey Avenue with the same group of badasses, lowlife's that would turn in their own granny for a buck, gangbangers with little or no respect for anyone or anything, especially an ex-cop. But what they did have was information about who was moving what on the street. People talk, and if you know who's listening, you can usually find out what you need to know; Shady Tree was a good listener.

I pulled up in the front of the house, a once imposing three-story structure built around the turn of the century but had seen better days. Sure enough, a half-dozen members of the gang were hanging around on the steps, just waiting for any kind of trouble that might happen by.

Shady, seated on the top step like some kind of urban warlord, looked the other way when he saw me. I figured

it was one of those, *"you don't see me if I don't see you"
kind of things.*

"Hey, Shady. You got a minute? Yeah, of course you
do. It's not like you wahoos have work to do, is it?"

Shady looked down at me, his eyes half closed, head
cocked to one side, the corners of his mouth twisted into
what I'm sure he thought was a fearsome sneer. The
dreads under the do-rag looked nasty and maybe full of
critters. It was that same old tough guy persona he
effected whenever he thought he had something to prove,
which was always.

*Why do these guys think that kind of crap scares
people?*

"Piss off, before you gets hurt, man," he growled.

"Now is that any way to treat an old pal, Shady? I
just want to have a little talk."

"You ain't welcome here," a guy sitting two steps
down from Shady said, playing with a butterfly knife.

I pulled back my jacket to show him my weapon, and
he looked away, eyes down.

"You think you can pull that mother before we take
you down?" The voice came from behind me. I turned to
see that I was surrounded.

"You want to try me?" I asked, resting my hand on
the grip.

"You ain't worth it, old man," the smallest of them
said.

"Sit d'hell down an' shut d'hell up," Shady snarled at
them.

They sat, looked away.

"Sorry about your kid, Shady," I said. "I'm trying to find out who killed him and was kind of hoping you might help me."

Shady looked uncomfortable like I've never seen him before. His eyes rolled as he looked at each of his friends like he was considering it, but daren't show any weakness in front of them. He shifted, stood up, shoved his hands into his pants pockets, sauntered slowly down the steps, stopped in front of me, his face so close to mine I could smell his breath; surprisingly, it smelled quite sweet.

"He dead becuz o' you, shithead." He turned his head sideways and without losing eye contact with me, spit on the ground then turned and walked away.

There was something about that look he'd given me that told me he wanted me to follow him, but to be discrete about it.

"You punks have a nice day," I said as I pushed past the crowd and got in my car and drove away in the opposite direction.

I made a left around the block and then left again onto a narrow access lane that ran behind the houses. Sure enough, there he was, and he didn't look happy.

I pulled up next to him, rolled down the window, and before I could yell for him to get in, he was in, slammed the car door closed and ducked down so he couldn't be seen. I took off down the street and out of the neighborhood.

"I only be here for Stitch," he said, sitting up in the seat. "I don't want nuttin' to do wich you."

"Got it. What do you know about what happened to him?"

"I know *you* ain't gonna touch 'em. They be way outa your league."

"What do you mean?"

"We talkin' heavy metal here, man. The big league. Ain't nobody gonna touch 'em. Not you, not the Feds. Look, man. I gotta go, befo' somebody see me. Pull over."

I did as he asked, and he opened the car door while it was still moving.

"Hold on, Shady. At least tell me who's running things or what it is they're running. Guns, drugs, what?"

He shook his and said, "You ain't even close... Just be careful, man," and then he turned and walked away.

What the hell was that supposed to mean, I thought, *not even close? Sheesh, that was a waste of time.*

All I knew now was that the operation was big and not some rinky-dink local gig. It wasn't much, but it was something.

I called Kate; no answer. I left her a message to call me. In the meantime, I had something else on my mind: Penelope and the Rose café. What the hell did they have to do with this mess? I needed answers, so that's where I headed.

I arrived there fifteen minutes later, all of my senses on high alert. That being so, the first thing I did as I parked the car was took a good look around. One thing that I hadn't noticed before really stuck out—all of the buildings around and next door to the restaurant were abandoned, boarded up. The café was a jewel in a pig pen. How come?

Hmm, I wonder... Maybe we should take a peek inside some of those. I'll check with Kate, see what she thinks.

I found a spot on the street in front of the café and parked the car. It was then I noticed something else: the Rose Café sign had been replaced by another that proclaimed the establishment to be Lucky's Diner.

I thought at first that the place was closed, but then I could see there were lights on inside, so I exited the car, pushed in through the front doors, looked around and...

"Hi! I'm Amber. Welcome to Lucky's Diner. You want a table?"

"Whoa! Where did you come from?" I was startled. I hadn't heard her coming.

"From the kitchen, of course. I'm sorry, I didn't mean to startle you. So, a table, then?"

She was a perky little thing in her late twenties: dark hair, bobbed; twinkling eyes and a crooked smile with teeth that looked as if they'd been bleached one too many times. She was wearing tight-fitting jeans, a white top under a short-sleeved jacket that did little to hide the tattoos on both arms; *Dragons*, I thought.

"No! No table... Lucky's Diner? What happened to the Rose Café?"

She shrugged. "The owners decided to make a change." Her crooked smile turned to an evil grin. "So, if you don't want a table, would you like something to go?"

I stared down at her. She didn't flinch; stared right back at me, daring me to argue with her. I didn't.

I looked around, over the top of her head, then said, "What about Penelope? Does she still work here?"

"Penelope? No, she doesn't work here anymore."

No shit, I thought sarcastically.

"Well," she said. "Can I get you something or not?"

"Yeah, you can tell me who owns the place. I'd like to have a word with them."

"I'm sorry," she said. "I don't have that information. What are you, a cop?"

I didn't answer. I stared at her.

She stared right back, then said, "Okay, I have work to do. So, if you're finished..."

"Yeah, I'm finished," I said. "Thanks for your help."

"You're welcome," she said and with a swish of her hips, she turned and hurried away into the kitchen.

I checked my watch. It was almost two o'clock. I stepped outside and looked around. The street was quiet. I decided to check out the vacant buildings on either side of the restaurant.

The red brick building to the right had several broken windows, faded and grimy, too high off the ground to look through. The front door was solid wood with several latches and locks. There was no way to get through them without an ax or electric saw.

I walked around the side of the building looking for another entrance or even a crack to see through, but there were none. I turned the corner at the rear of the building and found myself in a back alley that ran parallel to the two streets. It was littered with garbage cans, stacks of cardboard boxes, even the skeleton of a stripped car, its wheels long gone, its hubs resting on blocks. A metal door at the rear of the building was also locked up tight, and there were no windows at all in the alley.

There was a half-size dumpster at the back of the café; the kind used by restaurants to dump uneaten food and other waste. I lifted one of the lids; it was full. On top of the pile were two Rose Café menus, one on top of the other. I took a transparent evidence baggie from my pocket, stuffed my hand inside it, turning it into a glove of sorts, then grabbed the two menus by the corner and lifted them out of the dumpster. My thought was that maybe we could get some useful prints off of them.

I lowered the lid and was startled yet again. Amber was standing on the other side of the dumpster, staring at me.

"If I'd known you were that hungry, I'd have made you a sandwich," she said, but she wasn't smiling. "What's that you have in your hand?"

"Old menus," I said. "I'm a collector. Always looking for interesting... things in the garbage." I smiled my own evil smile.

My phone rang and my hand fumbled in my pocket to shut off the ringer. Amber was here for a reason, and I didn't think it was to empty the trash from the bathroom; I wanted to know what it was.

"Well, time's a-wastin'," she said. "If you're done collecting, you should go... *Now!*"

The smile was cold, the threat implicit, and she backed it up by brushing aside her jacket for me to see the grip of what looked suspiciously like a Ruger LCR .38 revolver.

"Well then," I said, lightly. "I won't waste any more of your time," and started to turn and walk away. I figured it was a no-win situation, not worth the hassle.

"The menus," she said quietly. "Put 'em back where you got 'em."

I turned back, smiled at her, lifted the lid, and slid the two menus back inside the dumpster.

"If you want to stay healthy," she said, leaning forward slightly, "you should keep your nose out of where it doesn't belong. Don't come back, y'hear?"

I didn't answer. I turned away and walked on down the alley to the next building where I stopped and turned to look at her; she was gone.

That building was boarded up too, but there were a few broken slats that provided me with a look inside. It was dark with lots of cobwebs and dust. There was nothing in there except maybe a few rats and cockroaches.

I thought about what Amber had said. *The bitch knew a whole lot more than she was telling me. She was packing. Since when did waitresses carry?*

My phone rang again. I looked at the screen. It was Kate. I answered it.

"Hey," she said. "Where are you?"

"I'm... It's a long story. How about you meet me at my office in say, an hour, and I'll tell you everything?"

"Okay, I'll wrap up here and head back to town. What's the address?"

I gave it to her and ended the call.

I rounded the corner back onto Third just in time to see a cop giving me a ticket.

"Hey, it's a legal parking zone."

She looked up from her pad and pushed back her hat a little. "Your license plate's missing. Lemme see your ID."

"Aw hell! Not again." I handed her my driver's license.

She walked back to her cruiser. Two minutes later she was back and handed me my license. "Get the license plate taken care of, Mr. Starke," she said as she handed me the ticket. She tipped her hat at me, got into her cruiser, and drove away.

Damn!

18

I drove to Enterprise on West 20th and rented a car. I left the Maxima with them, promising to return in a couple of days with a new license plate, and then I drove downtown to Georgia Avenue and my new office. I found it easily enough and was impressed. We had a ground-floor suite at the end of the block complete with a small parking lot big enough for maybe a half-dozen cars surrounded by a gated security fence. The gate was open so I drove in, parked, and entered through a side door: neat. Ronnie had done well.

"Hey, Ronnie. How are things coming along?"

"Pretty good, I think, so far. What d'you think of the place?"

"From what I've seen, I like it."

He beamed. "Great. So, we've set up desks—all, but yours, since I figured you'd want to pick out your own furniture—and we need to order a table for the conference room. I'm going to leave that to Jacque... I love her.

She's amazing. Love the accent. She's Jamaican. Did you know? Where the hell did you find her?"

I laughed. "Would you believe at my doctor's office? She's one of his patients. I paid her bill... That reminds me: see that she has some cash. I have a feeling she's just about broke; Tim too. Where are they, by the way?"

"Jacque's gone to Staples to get supplies. Tim's in the back office. He grabbed it for his own. You've no objection, right?"

"Of course not. What's he up to back there?"

"Who the heck knows? He's damn brilliant. I can't understand half of what he says. Our visit to Best Buy was quite the adventure. He's ordered desktops for me, Jacque and someone else yet unknown and yet to be hired. He was thinking ahead, I guess—a printer and some other bits and pieces, and a MacBook and an iPad for himself, but the rest of what he needs he has to order: servers, routers, monitors and God only knows what else."

Ronnie stopped talking for a second and chuckled. "He's gonna cost you a small fortune before he gets done, but I think it'll be worth it. The kid's a genius... Hey, you want to see your office?"

"Sure. Show me."

"It's right here, in the corridor, just off the main office." He opened the door and stood aside for me to go in, which I did.

It was big and bare, but I immediately fell in love with the great stone fireplace at the far end of the room.

"Hey, you two," Kate said. "What's going on? Wow,

nice office, Harry. Very upmarket... Well, it will be when I get done with it."

"When you get done with it? What the heck does that mean?"

"Well, you're obviously going to be busy, so I'll decorate it for you if you like."

I nodded, thoughtfully, and said, "Oh-kay..."

"Great," she said. "Tomorrow's Saturday. I'll make a start in the morning. What sort of budget do I have?"

"Whatever it takes, girl, whatever it takes... Kate, you're working. What about the case?"

"It's kind of stalled. You know how it is, Harry. We spend more time waiting for the experts: DNA, FBI... I'll take a couple of vacation days and get it done."

I shrugged. "Okay, if you think Henry will go for it."

"Harry, I'm owed more than forty days. He'll go for it."

"If you say so. Okay, so Ronnie and Tim you already know. Jacque will be back soon and I'll introduce you to her. In the meantime, I'll fill you in what happened after I left you guys." And I did. I told them first about my visit with Shady.

"Shady gave you information willingly?" Kate asked skeptically.

"No, just the opposite. He told me he wouldn't give me any info, just that organized crime was involved and that the guys running whatever it was were untouchable. It wasn't much, but it *was* something."

"Sounds like Shady," Kate said. "So do you have any idea what or who we're dealing with?"

"No, but if he's right, it's big, and we need to find out what it is and quickly, before anyone else dies. I'm thinking it's about the money Marsh scammed and they're using Phoebe as leverage. Ronnie, go get Tim. I need you two to work together and find out."

He went to find Tim, and Kate and I went out into the main office. I sat on the edge of one of the desks and Kate on one of the chairs.

Ronnie came back a minute later with Tim in tow with a laptop in one hand and an iPad in the other.

"Sit down, both of you," I said. "Tim, I need you and Ronnie to get to work. Is that laptop capable of doing what you need until you get the good stuff?"

He grinned, poked at the bridge of glasses, looked at Kate, blushed, nodded and said, "It depends what you need. It's not ideal, but for now, I'll do what I can."

I nodded. "Good." I turned to Ronnie. "What d'you know about Frank Marsh?"

"Not much more than you. I know he was an investment banker and that he ran several successful hedge funds."

I noticed that Tim had his iPad open and was typing notes into it.

"His main claim to fame though," Ronnie continued, "was his 'High Yield Investment Portfolio' which was an extremely sophisticated Ponzi scheme."

"What exactly are we talking about here?" I asked.

Ronnie nodded, looked at Tim who grinned at him, then said, "Ponzi schemes can be fairly complex, even when operated on a small scale, which Marsh's wasn't; he took his investors for more than one hundred million bucks before he got caught.

"It works like this: one person, sometimes a single group, coordinates every aspect of the scheme. That coordinator convinces numerous victims that they're investing in a legitimate investment fund with promises of big returns. Most offer unbelievably high returns of twenty percent and up, but Marsh was smart. He didn't do that. He guaranteed an ROI—return on investment—of fifteen percent. Pretty good, but still impossible to maintain in today's economy. Four or five percent would have been achievable."

Tim typed furiously on his iPad, soaking up all the details. Now that we were in the office, the geek seemed to be in his element.

Ronnie continued, "Well, anyway, the Ponzi scam artists are constantly on the hunt for new investors. They use the new investment money to pay dividends to the existing investors, and it works, at least for a while. For the scam to continue to work indefinitely, the coordinator would need to have access to an infinite supply of new investors... and that's where, sooner or later, it falls apart. The supply of new investors runs out and funds dry up, as happened with Marsh and, to a much greater extent, Bernie Madoff.

"When that happens, the investors lose everything they put into it and, if he's smart, the person running the scheme liquidates and leaves—vanishes before anyone can figure it out. Marsh got caught, but the money is gone. Where it's gone to is the big mystery. I think it's probably invested off-shore, in untraceable shell companies. Tracking those down is going to be a problem."

I looked at Tim. "What d'you think?" I asked.

"I think it will take some time, but it's not impossible. This," he said and looked at the laptop, "is not up to it, but my servers won't arrive until Tuesday, so it will have to do for now."

"Can we hurry it up?" I asked.

He looked a little perplexed, did his thing with his glasses, looked up at the wall clock, then took out his phone and made a call.

"Hey, Jerry," he said into the phone. "Look, I need that equipment like yesterday. Can you overnight it for me? I'll pay the cost... Okay, that's cool. You'll send me a bill? Great. Thanks, Jerry."

He ended the call, looked up at me and said, "Monday, by ten o'clock. That's the best he can do. EPB will be here around five this afternoon to install the Wi-Fi, and it will take me an hour to set everything up on Monday, so I should be up and running by eleven, eleven-thirty at worst. That's the best I can do."

I nodded slowly, looking at him, thinking how fortunate I was to have attended Ronnie's poker game where I met him. I had a feeling the kid was going to be my greatest asset.

"It will do fine, Tim. In the meantime, do what you can with what you have. Here's what we need to know..."

I thought for a minute while Tim watched, poised over his iPad.

"Okay, I want to know everything there is to know

about Frank and Phoebe Marsh, his Ponzi scheme, a list of investors, and I want you to try to track down the money. That's priority one. I'm thinking that maybe Phoebe is the key to this thing."

I paused, then continued, "Find out everything you can about a thug named Joseph James. He uses JoJo or JJ. I want to know who he works for, where he lives, the works. The same for one Benny Brown, late of this world, found dead in Ronnie's car."

I stopped for a second to make sure Tim was keeping up. He was.

"Find out all you can about the dead waitress, Penelope Ross and, if you can, what her connection is to the case, and to... Okay, that brings me to the Rose Café, now Lucky's Diner. Who owns it? I think it's a front for something illegal, human trafficking, maybe. I met another waitress there. Her name was Amber. I think she's much more than a waitress. See what you can dig up on her."

Again, I had to pause and think back over the past couple of days.

"There was a guy in the Sorbonne: small mouth, no forehead, a thug. It was him that snatched Phoebe Marsh. I need to know who he is and who he works for. I don't know how you'll pull that off... Hell, I'll go talk to Laura, maybe she knows who he is. Finally, there's money from the Ponzi scheme. We need to find—"

I was interrupted by the side door opening and a tight rear end clad in skin-tight jeans pushing inside.

"Okay, Tim," I said. "That will do for now."

A female voice with a Jamaican accent called out,

"Hey, can somebody please help me get all this stuff in outa my car?" Jacque turned around, a large cardboard box in her arms.

She dumped the box right next to me on the desk and said, "Hey, boss, if you wouldn't mind, please get your ass off my desk." She looked at Kate. "Who's this?"

I laughed and introduced them, then Ronnie and Tim went outside with her and began bringing in box after box of... I never did find out.

"So," Kate said, "it begins, your genesis from cop to PI. I'm proud of you, Harry."

I smiled at her. I was kind of proud myself.

19

I spent most of the weekend at my new offices. The place was a hive of activity. Kate and Jacque spent Saturday morning together shopping for office furniture, mostly for what was to become known as my lair, but also for filing cabinets, two more desks and chairs for the outer office, and a fancy handmade conference table and chairs... and a whole lot of other stuff I won't bore you with. Suffice it to say that by the time Monday morning rolled around, the place had gone from bare bones to a fully functional business office.

Me, I didn't spend much time there, not because I would have been in the way, which I would have been, but because I had three murders and a kidnapping to solve. I was antsy and needed to get on with it so while the girls were doing their thing, I hunkered down with Ronnie and Tim, brainstorming mostly.

By four o'clock that afternoon, I'd had enough; I gave it up. I had it in my head that Phoebe was the key to solving the case. I had to find her. To do that, I had to find Small Mouth, the guy who grabbed her that night at the Sorbonne, and that meant I needed information. I needed to know who the hell he was and who he worked for.

Goliath—JoJo James—was also a possibility, but I didn't know where to find him either. Well, at least I had a photo of him. But there was an inherent problem with that too; I knew he killed Stitch. I'd seen him do it. I also figured him for Penelope's murder. And I'd already made myself a promise: when I found him, I was going to kill him, after I drained him of everything he knew, of course. I took out my iPhone and opened the photo, stared at his ugly mug for several minutes, shook my head, and put the phone away.

And then there's Benny Brown, I thought. *Who killed him and stuffed him in Ronnie's trunk, and why? Was it connected to Frank Marsh and his Ponzi scam? If it was, was he killed just to frame me or, unbelievably, Ronnie? If so, it was a pretty weak effort. Even the new kid, Tim, had been able to see through it.*

And there was one more thing niggling at the back of my brain: what part was Shady Tree playing in the grand scheme, if at all? If he was involved, who was *he* working for? They killed his kid. I couldn't believe even he would lie down for that. Even so, I knew him well enough to know that if there was an easy buck to be made, Shady would find a way to shove his slimy fingers into the pie.

It was a lot to think about and I needed a place to start, or should I say a whom? *And who,* I thought, *would be better than my old friend, Benny Hinkle? That fat little bastard has his ear so close to the ground it's a wonder he doesn't get it stepped on... or at least kicked.*

I knew the Sorbonne opened for business at four o'clock. I also knew that the place would be deserted at that time of day, any day. I wanted to talk to Benny Hinkle, and Laura too, if she was there. Early afternoon, before four, would be the best time to do it. I was hoping those security cameras in the darkened corners of the bar were just that, security cameras and not fakes just for show.

I made arrangements to meet with Kate later that evening. Then I drove my rented car to Prospect Street, a dismal alley that gave access to the rear entrance of the Sorbonne, the same one where Small Mouth had abducted Phoebe, and I parked close by.

I locked the car and stepped up to the ill-maintained —rusty, paint peeling—steel door, thumbed the bell push, and waited, and I waited, and I pushed it again. *Damn it, Benny. Come on.*

Finally, I heard the locks being turned and the door opened an inch. Two beady eyes peered out at me. I sighed, shook my head, put a hand on the door, and pushed, hard.

Benny staggered back, squeaking with indignation.

"Damn it, Starke. What you doin' using the back door? Why'd you not come in the damn front door, like any other civilized dumb ass?"

Any other time I would have slapped his silly face for him, but I needed him to be cooperative, so I played nice.

"I didn't want to be seen coming in here, Benny,

okay? Lighten up a little. I just want to talk to you. You got a few minutes?"

He looked at me, frowning, then nodded somewhat mollified, I thought, then stood back and allowed me to walk through. He slammed the door behind me and locked it.

"There's no one in the bar, not yet. We'll go in there, c'mon."

I followed him as he waddled along the dark corridor past the restrooms and into the bar; more than ever he reminded me of Danny DeVito playing Louie De Palma in the TV show *Taxi*. He even had some of the same mannerisms.

I'd been in that bar more times than I could count and it was always the same... only this time it wasn't. It took me a couple of minutes to realize what was different: no loud music. *Thank God for that,* I thought, waving a hand at Laura who was behind the bar cleaning glasses.

Louie, I mean Benny, led me to a booth and we sat down opposite each other.

"Okay, Harry," Benny said, leaning forward, placing his elbows on the table and clasping his hands together in front of him. "Talk to me... No wait, you're not a cop anymore. I don't have to talk to you now, do I?"

"You're right, Benny, I'm not a cop anymore. I'm a private investigator, and no, Benny, you don't have to talk to me. But haven't I always treated you nice, and Laura too? Where is she, by the way... Oh, never mind, I see her. And would you like me to continue treating you nice? The alternative could be—shall we say—painful?"

He shook his head, tiredly, caught the drift of what I'd just said, looked sharply at me, and said, "Private investigator? You're kidding me, right?"

I shook my head, saying nothing.

"You're serious?"

I nodded, saying nothing.

"Frickin' hell, Harry. Who you think you are, Sam frickin' Spade?"

"Stop it, Benny. Are you going to help me or not?"

He grinned at me, leaned back on his seat, his hands still together on the table, and said, slyly, "What's in it for me?"

I stared at him for a long moment, my eyes narrowed, my lips clamped together, slowly shaking my head. He got the message.

He leaned forward again and said, "Okay, seein' as it's you. What d'you want to know?"

"Last Wednesday; we played poker, remember?"

He nodded.

"There was a girl, remember her?"

He thought, then nodded and said, "Yeah. I remember. What about her?"

"Do you know who she is?"

He shook his head. "Should I?"

"No, but she was snatched out back, and I'm trying to find her."

"You never said anything 'bout nobody bein' snatched."

"No, well, I thought maybe... ah, never mind what I thought. The guy who grabbed her was sitting at the bar, a mean-looking dude, small mouth, big forehead, broken nose. Do you remember him?"

"Yeah, he followed you in. I thought at first he was with you, but he sat at the bar, had a couple of drinks, and he must have left, but I didn't see him go."

"Who is he, do you know?"

"I seen him a couple times, well, several times. Usually there are two of 'em. Him and JoJo James."

I stared at him, barely breathing, trying not to show my elation.

"Oh yeah?" I said. "And who's he, this JoJo... *James?*"

"I don't know who your guy is, but if he's running with JoJo, I'd say he's a hard case. JoJo is a freelance enforcer, muscle."

I took out my phone, opened the photo I'd taken of James and showed it to Benny.

"This guy, right?"

He took the phone from me, stared at it, smiled and said, "You do this to him?"

I nodded. "Tough he might be, but he passed out at the sight of his own blood."

Benny looked nervously around, then said, "You'd better go, Harry. I don't want no trouble, and this guy is *trouble.* I swear to God: you did this to him—he's after you big time."

"I can handle him. Who's he working for, Benny?"

"I don't know, Harry. Really—I don't. I told you, he's freelance, works for anybody who'll pay his price."

"And you think they're working together, JoJo and Small Mouth?"

He shrugged. "Who's to say? But if they're spending time together..."

I nodded, thought for a minute, then said, "And you've never seen the girl before?"

"I didn't say that. She's been in several times. Not lately, but usually she's with a bunch of kids: students, I reckon. It's been... Hell, I dunno... a year, anyway, maybe longer."

That tallied with what Phoebe had told me. Well, she'd told me she knew the place.

"What about her dad, Frank Marsh? You know anything about him?"

"Are we talking about *the* Frank Marsh, the investment banker that screwed all those folks? If so, no, nothing. I feel for the kid, though. Can't be fun having to handle that kind of crap."

I nodded, couldn't help but agree with him.

"One more question, Benny, and I'll let you get back to whatever it was you were doing. What do you know about Benny Brown?"

He shrugged. "Used to come in here often. Not so much lately. Small-time player, mostly drugs. Don't know if he still does, but he used to work for a friend of yours." He paused, grinned at me and said, "Shady Tree."

"Holy shit, Benny. Are you serious?"

"Now when did I ever lie to you, Harry?"

I was stunned. I'd been a cop for ten years and was used to being surprised. In my line of work, you never can tell what's just around the corner. That one, though, I hadn't seen coming, not at all.

I looked up at the camera in the corner of the room and said, "That thing work, Benny, or is it just for show?"

"Hey, Laura," he shouted across the bar. "Harry needs the tape for last Wednesday from the security system."

She nodded, turned, stooped down behind the bar, and came up holding a VHS tape. *You've got to be kidding me.*

"Thanks, Benny," I said, rising to my feet and fishing out my wallet. "If you hear anything, see anything... If either of those two should drop by, I want to know, soonest. Got it?" I dropped a Benjamin on the table in front of him.

He looked up at me, grabbed the bill without looking at it, and nodded. "You got it, Harry."

I nodded; he'd got it. I grabbed the VHS tape from the bar top, and I got out of there. I had a lot of thinking to do, and a certain fine lady cop to wine and dine. With that, and what I'd learned, I figured it was going to be a good weekend, what was left of it.

And it was.

I was at my office by seven-thirty that following Monday morning and was surprised to find I wasn't the first to arrive. Hell, they were all there before me.

Ronnie had grabbed a vacant office and was setting up his computer. Jacque was bustling around organizing the front office. She'd even found herself an assistant, her thinking being that she had to spend time in the mornings at school and there needed to be a warm body to keep things together while she was away. I couldn't do anything but agree with her. So, Suzy Kennedy became the warm body and Harry Starke Investigations' fourth employee.

Tim... his mother had dropped him off—*I have to get that boy a ride*—and was already waiting when Jacque arrived. What the hell he was doing in his darkened cave at the far end of the suite I had no idea, nor did I want to, just so long as he could do what I needed when I needed it done. And after my talk with Benny Hinkle, I now had some solid leads that needed to be followed up. I went to talk to him.

He was sitting cross-legged on his chair, his hands together in his lap, eyes closed, in front of his laptop.

"Hey, Tim."

He came to with a jerk, almost fell off the chair. "Whuh, whuh, what is it?"

"Am I interrupting?" I asked as I pulled up a chair and sat down beside him.

"Er, no sir, Mr. Starke. I was just thinking. I've been trying to... Well, this thing—he waved a hand at the laptop—isn't up to what I need. My servers should be here by ten and then—"

"It's okay, Tim," I said. "Don't sweat it. There's no point in fooling around if you don't have the tools you need. Just hang loose for a minute. There are some things I need you to run down for me, but not until you have your equipment up and running, okay?"

He nodded, and I proceeded to fill him in on what I needed and finally, handed him the VHS tape from the Sorbonne.

"See what you can do with that, Tim."

His jaw dropped; he looked at it like I'd just dropped a scorpion into his palm.

"Wow," he said, turning it over and over. "I haven't seen one of these since... Mr. Starke, I'm gonna need someone to run me home. I have an old VCR if my mom hasn't tossed it out. And I know I should have cables, somewhere."

"Okay, just ask Ronnie to have someone take you. Do it now, Tim, before your gear arrives."

I really must get the boy a ride of his own, I thought, for the second time in less than ten minutes.

All that didn't take long. When I was done, I still had an hour to waste until I could go get a new license plate for my car, so I spent the hour drinking coffee, wasting everybody's time, and generally getting in the way. Jacque finally had enough and kicked me out so she could get done and away to school. At nine forty-five I checked out of the office, told Ronnie where I was going and that I'd be back in an hour.

Fortunately, the Tag and Title office is located just a couple of blocks away from my new offices at the County Courthouse on Georgia Avenue. All I needed to get a new plate was my ID and last tag receipt, which I'd found after a lengthy search of my home office late Sunday afternoon, so I was all set...

Oh yeah, I was all set. I'd forgotten it was getting close to the end of the month. I should have done my time-wasting at the courthouse.

By the time I got there, the place was packed. What a nightmare. There must have been sixty, or seventy, seats in the waiting area, and every one of them was occupied; it was standing room only. I took a number and settled in for a long wait. I opened up my iPhone and logged into Safari. I figured I'd do a little research into what qualifications I needed to make my new status official.

"Harry? Harry Starke?"

A hand touched my shoulder. It was Lawton Eider,

elder statesman and senior county commissioner, a legend in his own mind and one-time Democratic primary hopeful for the United States Senate. Unfortunately for him, it was Harold Ford Jr. who won the Democratic nomination meaning Eider would have to wait a few more years before he could try to unseat the incumbent Senator Bob Corker; good luck with that. Eider was old Chattanooga money, so he was down for a while but never out. He was a weak politician but still had a lot of connections, some not so good.

He was in his early sixties, tall and thin, with gray hair, a brush mustache to match, and wearing a light gray suit that I was certain didn't come from the Men's Warehouse.

I looked up. "Good morning, Ducky," I said, standing up, reluctantly. "How are you?"

He cringed. I knew he didn't like the nickname but what the hell, I didn't like Eider either. The nickname had been laid on him by a high school bully, a reference to the waterfowl of the same name, and it had stuck. He offered me his hand. I shook it, again reluctantly. He wasn't one of my favorite people.

"Well, I was just taking care of some county business when I saw you waiting in line," he said. "There's nothing I like better than doing a favor for one of our boys in blue. Let me take you to the front of the line."

Ducky was one of those politicians that liked to show off who he knows and what he can do for you.

"Thanks, but I'm no longer on the force."

"Oh," he said, his eyes wide with hope. "It wasn't an injury that took you off, I hope."

"No, just time for a change."

"Well, let me do you this one little favor for all the good things you've done for Chattanooga. It doesn't matter whether or not you're still on the force. You've earned it." His Southern drawl was thick, and he oozed with the charm of a used car salesman.

Any other time I wouldn't dream of taking a favor from Ducky Eider—because he'd want it back tenfold down the road—but waiting five hours in line for a car tag wasn't how I wanted to spend the rest of my Monday morning. I had things to do. And I had a feeling that time might be running out for Phoebe Marsh... if it hadn't already.

"That would be nice of you," I said, "but..." I hesitated for a second, then gave it up. "Well, okay. Thank you, Ducky; I appreciate it."

Again, he made with the cringe. But then he nodded, smiled, and walked me to the front of the line where a pretty redhead in her forties was helping a customer.

"Pardon me, Sally. Would you be so kind as to take care of my friend here once you're done with this good gentleman?" He patted the man being serviced at the counter on the back like he was an old friend.

Geez, I thought. What a sleaze... I can't believe I'm doing this.

"Of course, Commissioner. It will be a pleasure." She smiled mechanically without humor. I had no doubt I wasn't the first.

He put a hand on my shoulder, squeezed it, smiled, his mouth making like a split potato, and said, "Is there anything else I can do for you, Harry?"

"No, thanks. I really appreciate what you did." *This is going to come back to haunt me. I just know it.*

"You never know, maybe one day you can do me a favor. What are you going to do with yourself, by the way?"

And there it is.

"I'm going into business for myself," I said reluctantly.

"Oh, how absolutely interesting. What will this enterprise entail?"

"Private investigations. I'm going to be a PI."

"Something in the look he gave me made me feel what I was telling him was old news, but that couldn't be. Only a handful of people knew about my plans.

"You're not surprised?" I asked.

"Of course not. Why would I be? You are, after all, a great detective, are you not?"

"Well, I wouldn't put it like—"

"Oh come, come, Harry," he interrupted me. "Of course you are. Your closing rate is second to none. Something like eighty-two percent, if I'm not mistaken."

"How did you know that?" I asked.

"I try to stay on top of things, as my job as commissioner requires, Harry... Uh oh, you're up, and I have important things to do. Glad I could help in my small way. Keep the faith, Harry; keep the faith." He slapped me on the shoulder and was gone, just like that.

The customer at the counter finished, and I stepped up to the counter. The person in line behind me looked more than a little peeved that I had cut in front of him.

"Sorry," I said. "Official business; can't be helped."

To be honest, I felt guilty. Cutting in was something I'd never do, but five hours... I sucked it up and persuaded myself that... Nope, I still felt bad about it.

Sally smiled and said, "What can I do for you today?"

"Somebody stole my license plate. I need to replace it."

"Goodness me. That's quite a pickle to be in. It was darn fine luck that Ducky was here to help you up to the front of the line. I know you must be who you say you are if you're a friend of his. Nice man, Ducky. Fine upstanding politician."

He sure as hell has you fooled, I thought, smiling at her.

"Now, I know he can vouch for you." She looked around at her co-workers. "But do you happen to have any kind of ID on you, just for appearances, you understand?"

"Yup. Here's my, driver's license, police ID and... Is that enough? If not, I have my birth certificate."

"This will do just fine, and do you happen to have your last tag receipt? Excellent. Just give me a minute while I look you up. It says here your car is a Maxima. I just love Nissan. They make such fine cars. Now, would you like a vanity plate?"

"A vanity plate?"

I'd never thought of it before, but it would be kind of

cool to have something like one of those 70s TV detec-tives. *Yeah, right!* I thought. *I can just see me driving down the road with a plate reading "STARKE." I might as well put a target on the back of the car, saying "SHOOT ME."*

"No, thank you," I said.

She finished up the tagging and handed me the new plate and registration, and I left her to it. I smiled at the next guy in line and was gifted with a look that could have wilted grass.

I drove to Enterprise, turned in the rental, and a few turns of a screwdriver later I was legit once again. I checked my watch. It was just after eleven and, much as I disliked the man, I was grateful to Ducky Eider: he'd saved me at least a couple of hours.

21

I arrived back at my new offices a few minutes after eleven. I needed a coffee fix in the worst way and some time alone to think. The coffee was easy; the quiet time was not. I soon found out what it is to be in charge of a company. No sooner did I walk in the door than I was bombarded with questions, most of which I couldn't answer.

Fifteen minutes after I arrived, I was already missing Jacque. I needed a front man... Okay, okay, a woman... whatever. I needed Jacque to protect me from the minutia that came with running a business. *Damn. How long did she say it would be before she graduates? Next May? Wow!*

Anyway, I dodged most of the bullets and finally was able to go to my own office and shut the door, leaving instructions with the new girl—*hell, we're all new*—Suzy Kennedy, that I wasn't to be disturbed unless she received a message that my wife had died.

"But... you're not married. You don't have a wife."

"Exactly," I said, gifting her with a grin. "Keep 'em all away from me, Suzy, until I tell you differently, okay? And that goes for Ronnie and Tim too. Got it?" She had, so I made myself some more coffee and shut myself off from the world.

My office was still kind of bare. Ronnie had rustled up an old steel desk and a swivel chair I could use until we had something better, and Kate had found a couple of leather Chesterfield chairs in an antique shop. She'd ordered a proper desk—whatever that means—from a local cabinet maker, and that was it, except for a shiny new iMac computer on the desk.

I sat down, tapped the space bar and was immediately rewarded with the Google Chrome start page. I shook my head, clicked the sleep button, and turned the machine off.

I opened the desk drawer and found some yellow legal pads and a selection of colored pens, courtesy of Jacque, I was sure. Whatever, I set one of the pads on the desk and a red pen precisely aligned alongside it, and then I sat and stared at the pair. *Now what?*

I sat back in the chair and stared up at the light fixture, two bare bulbs in a black sconce. *That's gotta go. Hmm, I wonder how Tim's doing with his equipment?*

I almost did it; I almost got up and went to check on him, but I stopped myself. *You're here to think, dumbass. Now stop friggin' around and think... damn it.*

And that's what I did. I picked up the red pen and began to write. I made a short list of names:

. . .

Frank Marsh
    Marsh's Investors
    Phoebe Marsh
    JoJo James
    Small Mouth
    Penelope Ross
    Benny Brown
    Stitch Tree

THAT LAST MADE me sad and smile, both at the same time.

Then I had one of those weird feelings, and I added Shady Tree to the list. Why? *Benny Hinkle said that Brown had worked for Shady, so... So? Aw hell, I don't know! It'll come to me. It always does.*

The more I looked at the list, the more helpless I felt. When I was a cop, I had access to a whole world of law enforcement aids and resources: forensics, criminal databases, experts—even the medical examiner—on anything and everything. A few taps on the keyboard and it all lay at my feet. Not anymore. All of that was gone. All I was left with was my experience and brain to rely upon. The experience... yeah. The brain... hah!

It was at that moment I remembered the old saying that no man is an island, and I realized that I needed help.

I got up from my desk and shoved my head out of the door.

"Hey, Suzy. Ask Ronnie and Tim to join me in my

office, would you please? And"—I grinned to myself —"hold my calls." *I always wanted to say that. Now I can, whenever I want.*

"Grab a seat, both of you," I said when they arrived.

"Tim," I said, as I checked my watch. It was just after twelve-thirty; the morning had gotten away from me. "Did your equipment arrive okay?"

He nodded. "Yessir. You want to go see—"

"No," I interrupted him. "Not right now. Maybe later."

They sat down, and Tim set his briefcase on the floor beside him and opened his laptop on his lap.

"Look, I'm kind of stuck in a swamp here," I said. "I have no resources. When I was a cop, I could snap my fingers and get whatever I needed when I needed it. Right now, I need some answers. I need some help, and you two are it, I hope."

"What do you need, Harry?" Ronnie asked.

"JoJo James. I need to know who he's working for. Tim, have you had time to—"

"I did, I have. I ran his name through NCIC and—"

"You did what?" I interrupted him. I was stunned.

"I... ran his name through the National Criminal Information Center." He colored up. "Is that bad?" he asked, nervously, poking the bridge of his glasses with his finger.

"Yeah, it's bad," I said, glancing at Ronnie.

He was grinning like a fool.

"No," I said, "well yes, but... How the hell did you do that?"

Tim gifted me with a sly smile and said, "Same way I did the IRS."

"You hacked the NCIC database? You can't do that."

"Obviously, he can," Ronnie said, smiling.

I shook my head, thinking about the implications—and the consequences—of what I was hearing.

"Um, Mr. Starke," Tim said quietly, hesitantly, "I'm kinda confused. I'm a hacker. It's what I do. You know that. Isn't that why you hired me? Jacque, Suzy, Ronnie, any one of them can do data entry and Google searches, but I... I do what I do." He shut up and stared at me.

It hit me like a slap in the face. I may not have been aware of it at the time, but deep in my subconscious mind, it was exactly why I'd hired the kid.

I shook my head, then said, "You're right... You're right, Tim. That *is* why I hired you. I just didn't... Never mind. Just don't get caught, okay? If you do... Ah hell. Tell me what you found out about James."

"He has a record, of course, a long one, most of it petty stuff, but he was arrested for the murder of a drug dealer back in 1997 and again for the murder of a twenty-two-year-old prostitute in 2001. The charges, both of them, were dropped for lack of evidence, that and because he had alibi's both times. As far as I can tell, he doesn't work for anybody per se. He freelances. I still need to do a little more digging, though. Is that okay?"

I nodded. "Yes, well done, Tim. Just be careful. I don't want us to get shut down before we even get started." I paused, then said, "How about Small Mouth? I need to know who he is and who he's working for... Tim, did you have any luck with that tape I gave you?"

"Is this Small Mouth?" He turned the screen toward me. On it was what was obviously the first page of an FBI file with a mug shot at the top left.

"How the hell did you find him?"

Tim grinned.

"I converted the images from the tape you gave me to digital—they weren't very good—and then I..." He paused, made a face, then continued, tentatively, "I ran it through the FBI's Computer Aided Facial Recognition Project, CAFRP... and there you are. His name is..."

I didn't hear the name. My head was spinning. *Holy Mary Mother of God,* I thought. *What the hell have I gotten myself into?*

I stared at him without seeing him. Inwardly, I was shaking my head in horror. I'd heard about CAFRP, but I didn't know it was in use. It was controversial even back then. I certainly didn't have access to such resources when I was a cop. Now, it seemed I did. *And will it be a blessing or a curse?* I wondered.

"I'm sorry, Tim," I said, very quietly. "What did you say his name is?"

"Amos Watts."

"And what do we know about him?" I asked, my curiosity gaining the advantage over my concern.

"Not much. He doesn't have much of a record, but he was a suspect in a bank robbery back in 2005, hence his likeness in the FBI database, but he was never charged. The

FBI does have a file on him though, and it seems they're keeping it up-to-date... Well, until the last entry three months ago, they were. He's suspected of being a mule for the Chupacabra Cartel, which is probably why they're keeping an eye on him. That's all they have... officially."

"How about unofficially?" Ronnie asked.

"Again, not much. I found a second file, a stray that someone had uploaded into the FBI system. It was written by a Border Patrol agent named Jose Ramos. It seems he, Watts, is also a coyote, involved in human trafficking across the Rio Grande, but again, there's nothing specific."

He paused, looked guilty, did that thing with his glasses, then stared defiantly at me and said, "Okay! Look, Mr. Starke, I know that he's running with... that he's involved with James."

"And how do you know that?" I asked, dreading the answer.

"Joseph James has an iPhone," he said, setting his laptop on the edge of my desk and reaching for his briefcase. "I hacked the phone company—actually, I hacked four of them before I found the right one—and got his phone records. There are several numbers he calls a lot, all the time, in fact. I pulled those records too. One of them belongs to Amos Watts."

"Phone records?" I asked, praying that I would still go to heaven.

"Yeah, I have a bunch. Will they help?" He handed me a sheet of paper.

"Oh yeah, they'll help." I looked down the list. Tim

was right. There were several dozen numbers he'd called often; three of them a whole lot more than often. I looked up at him.

"These three," I said. "Can we find out who they belong to?" I asked, by that time knowing full well that he could.

He grinned at me. "I thought you might ask that. Here you go." He handed me another single sheet of paper with a list of a half-dozen numbers with names thereon, and one number without a name, seven numbers in all. Then he handed me the matching phone records, and there was a pile of them.

I looked at the records. JoJo James had called one of the numbers—or had been called from the number— thirty-seven times over the past six weeks. Amos Watts had talked to the same number twenty-nine times, and to James almost as many. The other number, the one without a name, had forty-two calls listed to it.

Now that is *interesting!* I thought. But one of the names was even more interesting.

I wrote the name on a piece of paper and handed it to Tim. "I want to know everything there is to know about this guy."

Tim grinned at me, and said, "I thought you might say that. Here you go, boss." And he handed me several more printed sheets of paper stapled together at the corner.

I glanced at them and smiled to myself, then set them aside for later.

"You really do have a knack for this, kid, don't you?" I

said. "Is there any way to trace the nameless number?"

Tim sat there with a smile on his blushing face. "I'm working on it. It's a burner, but I already know it was purchased for cash at Walmart on Shallowford Road on September 10 this year at three-oh-nine in the afternoon. I need to hack into the security system. If they have a camera—knowing the time of purchase—I should be able to grab a copy of the video. If there's a good image of the buyer—"

"Okay, okay, Tim," I interrupted him. "I get it, and it's a whole lot more information than I need right now. Just do what you have to do and for Pete's sake, don't get caught."

Damn! I thought savagely. *Oh for the days when I could go get a warrant and just demand the security footage. Now I have to resort to— this?*

There was a knock at the door, it opened just enough for Suzy to stick her head inside.

"I know you said you were not to be disturbed, but there's a cop here, says her name is Sergeant Gazzara, that you know her. She looks upset. What do you want me to do?"

"Let her in." Before the words had come out of my mouth, Kate was through the door.

"What the hell's wrong with you, Harry? Hello, Ronnie, Tim."

Tim shot up out of his chair as if it was on fire, grabbed his laptop from my desk, and snapped it closed. He did not sit back down.

"Nice to see you too, Kate," I said. "What's up?"

"I just got a call from Henry Finkle. He received a call from Commissioner Lawton Eider and now he's on my ass. Eider's made a complaint about an incident, about your behavior, at the courthouse."

I frowned, confused. "Incident? What incident?"

"He said you pushed your way to the front of the line and insisted on being helped before anyone else. He said you said something like, "I'm a cop. I don't wait in line.""

Why wasn't I surprised? I looked again at the papers that Tim had prepared for me. I had an idea the answers I needed were already in my hands.

"He was lying," I said quietly. "He insisted on taking me to the front of the line. Said it was little enough to do for me after all I'd done for the city."

Kate put her hands on her hips. "Why would he lie?"

"You're asking me why a dirty politician would lie?" I said.

She pursed her lips, frowned, turned her back to me, and walked toward the fireplace.

Tim, still standing, piped up. "Um... hello again, Miss Gazzara. You look very nice today."

Kate was completely taken off-guard, as was I, but I couldn't help smiling. *Geez, I love this kid.*

Tim was right, though. She'd gone home after she'd left me and changed clothes. She was wearing jeans and a white roll-neck sweater under her signature tan leather jacket.

She turned, looked at him, her eyes narrowed. She took a deep breath and sighed. "Thank you, Tim." Then she looked at me and said, "Why would he do that, Harry? Lie about something so... petty. It's stupid."

I smiled at her; I knew something she didn't.

"Not so stupid as you might think," Ronnie said, looking at Tim. "Show him the list, Tim."

Tim handed me two sheets of paper stapled together and said, "This is a list of the major investors, or should I say, victims, in Frank Marsh's Ponzi scheme."

I took it from him and glanced down the list... actually, I didn't. The name I was looking for was only three down from the top of the list. I stared at it, almost unable to comprehend what I was seeing.

"Three-point-four million dollars," I said, without looking up. "I'd say that's just about wiped him out."

"What?" Kate asked. "Who are you talking about?"

"Lawton Eider," I said.

"Tim," I said. "I need to know who owns that burner phone and I need to know now. Can you—"

"I'm on it," he said, already heading for the door with his briefcase and laptop in hand. "It might take a while." He rushed out into the corridor, leaving the door wide open.

"Sit down, Kate," I said, nodding at the chair Tim had vacated. "I think I know who's behind all of this."

"Well," she said, tapping her foot. "Are you going to tell me or not? I'm assuming from what you just said about Eider that it's him, right?"

"I think so," I said. "I think it's all down to Eider. He's lost a ton of money, and he wants it back. But I'm still trying to figure it out. I need to know who owns the burner phone he's been calling. In the meantime, I also think he has Phoebe Marsh... if she's still alive. Can you..."

"You want me to come with you?" she asked, her eyes wide.

I nodded.

"Oh, I don't know, Harry."

"What's wrong?" I asked. "Is it your case?"

"No, not that. I'm still playing the waiting game—you know how the labs are. Bloodwork is easy, DNA not so much." She rolled her eyes. "I left Tracy to do the grunt work. He should be able to hold things together for a while. No, Harry, Eider is a county commissioner and we only have... What you have is all circumstantial."

"I know all that," I said. "But if I'm right, he does have Phoebe Marsh, or at least he knows where she is. He's using her to pressure Marsh. He wants his money."

"How do you know all this?" she asked.

"The phone records," I said. "James has been talking to Eider for almost two months, so has Watts... and Eider has talked to whoever has that burner more than forty times. These guys are badasses, Kate. What would a guy like Eider be doing with the likes of them? No good, that's for sure. James is freelance muscle, a killer. Watts too, probably."

"It's one hell of a stretch, Harry. Just because he's been talking to some rough characters doesn't mean—"

"Rough characters?" I interrupted her. "I just told you, James is a frickin' killer. We know that because he killed Stitch—probably to stop him from talking to me. I saw him do it, and he knew I would come after him for it. I also think he killed Penelope Ross for the same reason, to stop her from talking to me. Then either he or Watts murdered Benny Brown and tried to frame me for it in a weak attempt to put me away, to stop me. I think Eider hired the two of them to kidnap Phoebe and use her to pressure Marsh into revealing where he stashed the money, almost one hundred million."

I paused, looked at her for a minute, then said, "Look, I can't do this on my own. I don't have the authority; you do."

She just stared at me, said nothing.

Come on, Kate, I thought. *What the hell are you thinking about?*

I tried one more thing. "And then there's this," I said, handing her a sheet of paper. "I asked Tim to find out who owns the Rose Café, now Lucky's Diner. Check it out."

She read for a moment then looked up at me and said, "I don't believe it."

But I could tell from the look on her face that she did.

"It's true," I said, "and the place is mortgaged up to the rafters. Eider is in so deep he's drowning. I'm betting that Phoebe Marsh is being held at the café. Now, can you get a warrant to go search the place? Ask Henry Strange. He has a soft spot for you."

She gave me a look. "And what about the other Henry—Finkle? He'll lose his onions if I go chasing after a county commissioner. It's not my case, Harry. It's assigned to Eric Cable."

I was exasperated. It was the same old, same old all over again: office politics. I didn't think Kate played that game, but... it seemed she did.

"You know what, Kate," I said. "This is exactly why I got out. All the freakin' red tape, delay after delay, and in the meantime, there's a kid's life at stake. You do whatever the hell you want. I'm going to see Eider. Then I'm going to take the Rose freakin' Café apart, and James and Watts along with it if they get in the way, and maybe even if they don't. I promised Stitch's dead body I'd get James, and by God, I will."

"Okay, okay," she said, holding up her hands. "I'll call Judge Strange."

And she did, and fifteen minutes later we were on our way to the Federal Building to pick up the warrant.

22

W e made a quick stop by Judge Henry Strange's office to pick up the warrant. Then we headed for the county courthouse.

I ran up the courthouse steps, up the stairs to the third floor, and barged into Eider's outer office.

Kate identified herself to the receptionist and told her to leave and close the door behind her. Reluctantly, the woman stood, looked at Eider's closed door, then did as she was asked. I nodded my thanks to Kate, then flung open the door to the commissioner's office and strode inside.

He was sitting behind his desk tapping on a computer keyboard. To say he was startled by my sudden appearance in his office would be something of an understatement. He stood up, hands out in front of him as if to ward off the grim reaper, which I suppose I was.

"Ha-rry," he stammered. The color had drained from

his face. "It was just a joke—I swear. I'll call Henry Finkle and tell him, right now, okay?" He picked up his desk phone and leaned forward to dial.

"Sit the hell down, Ducky. This isn't about your stupid report, though I should bust your head for it. It's about Phoebe Marsh. Where the hell is she?"

He dropped down into his chair as if he'd been shot.

"Easy, Harry," Kate said.

"Easy my ass. If I don't get what I need, I'm going to take this son of a bitch apart. Now tell me," I said to Eider. "Where is she?"

"I don't know what you're talking about," he said, regaining some of his composure. "Who is Phoebe Marsh?"

I stared at him, slowly nodding my head, thinking, trying to figure out if I should talk to him or just take his head right off his shoulders. I opted for the first option.

I sat down in front of the desk. Kate also sat. I gathered my thoughts, then said, calmly, "There's no use denying it, Ducky. I have you dead to rights—"

"You have nothing," he interrupted me. "You don't have any right to talk to me about anything. You're not even a cop. Now get the hell out of my office before I call a real cop."

"That would be me," Kate said, cutting him off. "Sergeant Catherine Gazzara. This is my ID and this"—she waved the document in the air—"is a search warrant for this office and your other business."

She laid the warrant on the desk in front of him. He stared at it like it was a snake preparing to strike.

"What... other business?" he stammered.

"The Rose Café," I said. "Lately Lucky's Diner, only it ain't so lucky anymore. Now, can we talk, or do I have to get rough with you?"

"I want my lawyer," he said belligerently.

"Tough," I said. "I'm no longer a cop, remember? I don't have to play by the rules anymore so, you either talk to me or... I'll hurt you," I said, sweetly.

He stared at me, said nothing.

"I'll take that as a yes," I said, looking at Kate.

She was slowly shaking her head at me. I grinned at her. I was feeling pretty good. For the first time in ten years, I was in charge and didn't have to play by the rules. Good for me... Really tough for Ducky Eider.

"Now, Ducky," I said quietly, leaning forward, trying to look earnest, "I know you have two ugly—make that two nasty-assed sons of bitches working for you. One, Joseph James, also known as JoJo, or JJ, and two, a Neanderthal named Amos Watts. I know that they're working for you because I have your phone records and theirs. You want to comment?"

"I have no idea what you're talking about. I don't know any... JoJo whatever-his-name, nor anybody called Watts."

"Ah, Ducky. That won't fly. By the way, you should know I'm recording this," I said, holding up my iPhone for him to see. *It's a bit late to tell him now,* I thought. *Never mind, my bad!*

"It won't fly because I have a record of all the calls you made to them, and them to you, and there are a *lot* of them, some of them twenty minutes and longer, so you definitely do know them."

He didn't answer, but he was beginning to look very uncomfortable.

"I also know you had Watts abduct Phoebe Marsh. I know because I was there when he did it."

"You're out of your mind, Starke. Why would I do that?"

"Because you're broke, Ducky. Because Frank Marsh scammed you for every last penny you had—three-point-four million, to be precise, and you thought you could use Phoebe to pressure him into giving it back. But you were wrong, weren't you? Marsh wouldn't play, would he?"

He didn't answer, but I had a feeling he was weakening. It was time to hit him in the gut.

"Ducky," I said gently. "You're in so deep you're about to drown. You're not only up for kidnapping the girl, but we can also lay three murders at your feet. A young black kid, Stitch Tree; a witness, Penelope Ross"—that was a bit of a stretch, but I was on a roll—"and one slimy piece of work by the name of Benny Brown."

His eyes bulged. He slowly stood up, pointing at me, his hand trembling. "You-you, I... No, *NO!* I know nothing about any murders. The girl... yes, okay, I hired them to take her. You're right. I wanted my money back, but that's all. I had nothing to do with any killings, I swear it."

And you know what, I believed him. Better yet, I now had his confession to Phoebe's abduction, recorded.

"Mr. Eider," Kate said, rising to her feet and reaching for her cuffs.

"Just a minute, Kate," I said. "Let me finish."

She nodded and sat down again.

Eider looked at me, helpless, a duck out of water, if you'll pardon the pun. "I don't have her," he said. "I never did. I don't know who does. One of James' acquaintances, I think. I talked to him on the phone, but I never met him, and I don't know his name."

I believed that too. He was talking about the unknown burner phone.

"Where are James and Watts?" I asked.

"There's an apartment above the diner. I let them use it. It's where they're living."

I looked at Kate and nodded.

She nodded back, rose to her feet again, grabbed her cuffs, and said, "Lawton Eider, I'm arresting you for the kidnapping of Phoebe Marsh..." And she continued reading him his rights, then escorted him downstairs to a waiting police cruiser.

We stood for a moment on the courthouse steps and watched them take him away. Then Kate turned to me, smiled, and said, "Good one, Harry. You just solved your first case."

"I did, didn't I? How about that?"

"But you're not done, not yet."

"Nope; not yet. Let's go find Tweedledum and Tweedledee."

23

We climbed back into Kate's unmarked cruiser and together we headed for East Third and Lucky's Diner.

"You think I should call for backup?" she asked.

"No, not until we at least know they're there. We would want to look like a couple of fools, now would we?"

"Hah," she said, "Finkle would love that... Listen to me, Harry. I know you better than you know yourself. I know what you're thinking. You can't do it."

"Do what?" I asked, smiling.

"Kill James."

"I hear ya, Kate," I said, smiling inwardly. "That reminds me." I reached inside my jacket for my trusty M&P9, checked the load, and returned it to its home.

Kate sighed and shook her head.

We arrived at the front entrance of Lucky's at precisely three forty-eight that afternoon—I know because I happened to glance at the clock on her dash—to find the place deserted... except for two very large gentlemen—and I use that word loosely—seated together at the bar drinking coffee.

"Hi guys," I said, loudly. "How're they hangin'?"

"Oh shit!" I heard Kate whisper.

They both looked round over their shoulders. Watts leaped to his feet and over the counter and out through the kitchen. Kate ran around the end of the counter and went after him.

James sat still for a moment, staring at me. Then he smiled, stood, turned toward me, feet spread slightly, then he shrugged, twisted his head first one way then the other, his hands hanging loosely at his sides, bent slightly at the elbows. His coat was swept back to reveal what could only have been a .45 in a holster at his right hip.

Oh shit. What does he think this is, the OK Corral?

"Don't do it, JoJo," I said. "I'm faster than you. *Geez, did I really say that?*

He grinned at me. I watched his eyes and... there it was: his right eye twitched and his right hand moved. And so did mine, it swept up under my jacket, sweeping the gun from its holster and bringing it to bear in one silky swift move.

His gun had barely cleared leather when my bullet tore into his right shoulder, spinning him around, the heavy weapon falling from his hand. He staggered backward, staring at me, his eyes wide, looked down at his right hand and the blood dripping from it to the floor... and then he passed out.

So he really can't stand the sight of his own blood.

"Watts has gone," Kate said. "He ran out through the kitchen and out into the alley. He had a car. He was in and gone before I could stop him. How about you?" she asked, looking down at the unconscious JoJo James. "I told you not to kill him, Harry."

"He's not dead," I said. "He passed out again. He'll be okay. Better call for an ambulance though."

She nodded, made the call, and we waited until the EMTs had loaded JoJo up.

"Now what?" Kate asked as we walked back to her unmarked cruiser.

"We've got to find the kid before they decide she's no longer useful. I was hoping we could persuade one of them to tell us where she is but—"

I was interrupted by the ring tone of my iPhone. I checked the screen: "unknown number." I was just about to decline the call when something stopped me. Reluctantly, I took the call. I hadn't known him long, but I recognized his voice instantly.

"Oh, hey, Tim, it's you. What do you have for me?"

I listened.

"Okay," I said, then, "You're kidding! Okay! Okay... Got it, and thanks, Tim. You done good, son. I'll talk to you later." I disconnected, looked at Kate and said, "Let's go."

24

He was sitting on the steps with two of his henchmen. When he saw our car stop in front of the house, he jumped to his feet, ran down the steps and away up the street. I went after him, gun in hand; Kate followed. He didn't get far.

"Hey, Shady, you stupid son of a bitch," I yelled. "Stop, or I'll drop you."

He must have believed me because he slowed: the run became a jog, then a fast walk and then he stopped and slowly turned around to face me, walking backward, smiling.

"Hello, Harry," Shady Tree said. "I guess you figured it out, huh?"

I held the gun steady in both hands, my head cocked to one side. He shrugged, raised both hands to shoulder level. I lowered my weapon, took a step forward, and as I did, his right hand went for the gun on his hip.

You've got to be kidding me! The thought flashed

through my head as I brought my own weapon to bear. *Not twice in one day.*

It happened in slow motion... at least that's what it seemed like. His gun came up, and I pulled the trigger. The nine-millimeter copper-coated slug hit the meaty part of his right forearm, just below the elbow. His arm snapped backward, and the gun flew out of his hand and across the street. He looked at me, wide-eyed, unbelieving, shocked, looked down at his arm, then dropped to his knees, grabbed the wound and looked at me, pleading. Then it hit him, his head went back, his eyes squeezed tightly shut as the nerves registered the wound and the pain coursed through him.

I holstered my weapon and ran to him.

"You stupid son of a bitch," I said in his ear as I dragged his jacket off, and then tore off his shirt sleeve. "I could have killed you."

He was lucky. I could tell the bullet had missed the bone; what it might have done to tendons, muscles, and nerves, I had no idea.

"If it had been anybody else but me," I said, "you'd be dead right now. *And if I was still a cop,* I thought, *I'd be disciplined for not taking the kill shot.*

"Where is she, Shady?" I asked as I used the shirt sleeve to tie off his wound.

"Where's who?" he ground out through gritted teeth.

"You know who."

He howled as I gently squeezed the wound.

"Where's Phoebe Marsh?"

He looked up at me. I don't know if it was pain or hate I saw in his eyes. "Screw you, Starke."

"No, screw you, you piece of garbage." I squeezed the wound and Shady cried out as the pain intensified.

"Stop it, Harry," Kate said.

"Not until he tells me where she is," I said, looking him right in the eye. It was at that point Shady Tree became a believer.

"She's in the basement," he whispered, his eyes shut tight. "Under the floor, north corner. There's a section, looks like concrete, only it's made of something called vermiculite. It weighs nothing, comes up easy. Now, will you get me to the hospital?"

"She'd better be good and healthy, Shady," I said. "If not..." I didn't bother to finish. He knew. I could see it in his eyes.

"Kate," I said. "I'll go look. Keep an eye on him. Call an ambulance, if you like."

I ran back to the house. The gangbangers were gone. I guess they'd seen what had happened to their boss and decided to get going, fast. I ran up the steps, into the house, found the basement door next to the kitchen, opened it, and ran down the steps into the basement.

It was dark down there, even with the light on. I walked slowly through the garbage to the north corner and looked around the floor. At first, I didn't see anything and was about to go screw Shady's arm some more when I spotted the false concrete slab. It was about three feet square, dirty, stained, almost identical to the rest of the concrete floor. If I hadn't been looking for it, I wouldn't have found it.

I knelt down, ran my fingers over the smooth surface and edges, trying to find a way to get it up; nothing. I reached into my pants pocket, took out my tactical pocket knife, flipped it open, and inserted the tip of the blade into the crack that separated the slab from the rest of the floor. Then gently, I began to lever the slab, hoping to hell I wouldn't snap the blade.

But Shady was right. It took very little effort to raise the edge of the slab enough to get my fingers under it. I swear that slab didn't weigh five pounds.

I lifted it out and set it to one side, revealing a large square opening with steps leading down into the darkness.

I turned on my iPhone and used the flashlight to tentatively make my way down the first few steps, feeling my way as I went. Five steps down, on the side of a joist, I found a light switch. I flipped it on and descended the rest of the way into hell... at least that's what it must have felt like to Phoebe.

The room was small, no more than eight feet by eight. Phoebe was in a small cage set against the far wall... and when I say small, I mean tiny. She couldn't stand upright, she was on her butt, her knees pulled up to her chest, and she was filthy, and it also looked like she'd lost weight.

"What the hell took you so long?" she asked wearily.

"And hello to you too," I said, wondering how the hell I was going to get her out of the cage.

"There's a key," she said. "Hanging on the top step, to the right."

"Are you okay?" I asked as I pulled the cage door open. "They didn't..." *Because if they did, Shady is going to pay for it, like he's never known.*

"Yes, I'm okay, and no, they didn't. They didn't touch me."

"What took you so long?" she asked again. "You got my note, right? You talked to Penny, right? You must have because you're here."

"Penny? You mean Penelope, from the Rose Café?"

"Yes. She's my friend."

Oh shit.

"Let's get you out of here," I said, changing the subject and helping her out of the cage and to her feet. She was so stiff she could barely stand.

I guided her up the steps into the basement proper, and then up into the main house, where we found Kate coming in through the front door.

"Oh, my God," she said. "You found her. That's fantastic. Are you okay?"

Phoebe smiled at her as she limped into the kitchen and sat down at the table.

"Yes, I'm fine. Where is he, that SOB with the dreads? I wanna remove his... I wanna bust his balls."

"He's outside," Kate said, "with two uniforms watching him, waiting for the paramedics. Harry shot him."

"He's dying, right?" she asked gleefully.

"Not hardly," Kate said. "He should be, but Harry

only winged him. We need to get you to the hospital, get you checked out."

"Not until I've talked to Penny. Where is she? Can we go see her?"

I looked at Kate, then back at Phoebe. I didn't know what to say.

"Harry," Kate said quietly. "Why don't you go and finish up with Shady?"

I nodded, got up, and left them alone together.

25

Shady was sitting on the sidewalk, nursing his arm.

"Piss off, Starke," he said, looking up at me. "I don't want no more to do with you."

"I want to talk to you about Stitch," I said, crouching down beside him.

"I don't wanna talk about dat."

I shook my head, bewildered. "He was your son, Shady."

"I had nothing to do with it. Stitch, he liked her, the girl, talked to her, sometimes, told her not to worry. He was warned not to talk to nobody. JoJo was watching him at the laundry. Then you, of all people, turns up and Stitch gets in your car. He was warned. He got nobody to blame but hisself."

"But you, Shady. What about you? You must feel something."

"It be tough out here... Kids, they die all'a time. Don't

mean a whole lot o' nothin'," he said, but I could tell that it did.

Even Lester Shady Tree had a heart in there somewhere.

JOSEPH JOJO JAMES survived his wound and was charged with the murder of Benny Brown. CSI found trace evidence on Benny's body, and DNA, all belonging to JoJo. He was sentenced to life without the possibility of parole.

Amos Watts was arrested by Border Patrol agents in El Paso and was extradited back to Chattanooga, where he got lucky. He cut a deal with the DA, and friend of mine, Larry Spruce. He spilled his guts about Ducky Eider's crimes and got off with just five to ten years in state prison.

No one was charged with the murders of Penelope Ross and Stitch Tree. JoJo James had alibis for both murders and, for some reason, my word wasn't good enough to put him away for killing Stitch, but what difference would it have made? JoJo would never walk free again.

Shady... my man Shady. He also got five to ten for his part in Eider's crimes. If he was a good boy, he'd be out in 2013... My oh my.

Ducky Eider? It's kind of ironic, laughable even: he was convicted of conspiracy to kidnap Phoebe Marsh and sentenced to twelve years, federal. He's in the same prison, in Atlanta, two cells down from his old buddy, Frank Marsh.

Phoebe Marsh didn't take the news that Penny was dead very well. Apparently, the two were childhood friends, had attended the same schools together. Kate and I accompanied Phoebe to Penny's funeral. She didn't have much to say, didn't know what she was going to do. Then, a couple of months later, Kate told me that Phoebe had applied to the police academy and that she, Kate, had sponsored her. Nine months later, Kate and I attended her graduation and induction into the department.

Me? Kate and I spent a lot of time together the next two months: she working on my office, and... Well, she managed to rid herself of her new partner, Dick Tracy, and she successfully closed out her first case as lead detective. I did think, for a while that we might... That maybe...

So, I spent the next couple of months working my ass off putting my new company together, trying to get things working smoothly.

Tim settled in; cost me more money than I earned in a year at the PD. Oh, and I did buy him a car: I found him a neat little red MGB GT. I figured it suited his personality. Since then he's been insufferable, treating me like I'm his dad or something. I'm going to have to fix that somehow, but gently.

Jacque continues to brighten my every day, and Ronnie... well, Ronnie is Ronnie.

One thing of note did happen during those two

formative months: I hired Bob Ryan... but that's a whole nother story.

So, there you have it. That's the story of how I made my transfer from cop to private investigator. Over the next several months, I struggled a bit, trying to get a handle on running my own business and all the responsibility that comes with it. I handled a couple more cases, made some stupid mistakes, and... well, those are stories for another day.

HARRY STARKE

Thank you:

I hope you enjoyed reading this story as much as I enjoyed writing it. If you did, I really would appreciate it if you would take just a minute to write a brief review (just a sentence will do).

Reviews are so very important. I don't have the backing of a major New York publisher. I can't take out ads in newspapers or on TV, but you can help get the word out. I would be very grateful if you would spend just a couple of minutes and leave a review.

Credits:

My thanks to my editor Diane Shirke for doing a great job, as usual. What would I do with you, Diane? Thank you for all you've done make this book the best it could be.

My thanks also my law enforcement and firearms specialist friends. You're always there when I need you:

Ron Akers, Gene Flowers, David Young, CSI Laura Lane. Finally, I have to thank my wife, Jo, for putting up with me and my quirks and the long hours when I'm at the computer writing and therefore unavailable.

If you haven't already read them, you may also enjoy reading the novels in the original Harry Stark series. The first is, of course, Harry Starke. Here a sample of the book that began it all:

26

HARRY STARKE

I t was just after midnight. The only sound was the gale-force wind howling through the ironwork, blowing in off the river. The snow was almost a blizzard, small flakes flying fast, horizontal. It was cold. I was cold. I pulled up the collar of my overcoat, leaned over the parapet, and stared down into the darkness. The lights from the aquarium and the Market Street Bridge sparkled on the surface of the water.

Whitecaps on a river? This is no place to be. So, what the hell am I doing here?

A good question, and one for which I had no good answer. I'd spent the hours before midnight at the Sorbonne, a fancy name for a dump of ill repute, one of Chattanooga's sleaziest bars. I frequented it more often than I probably should, mostly to keep an eye on the lowlifes that inhabit the place. It's what I do.

Yep, I'd had a couple of drinks. Yes, really, it *was* only two, and no, I wasn't drunk. If you want to know the truth, I was bored, bored out of my brains watching the drunken idiots hitting on women they didn't know were hookers. At first it was kind of funny, then just pathetic. Finally, I'd had enough. I left the Sorbonne a little before twelve. The company had been bad, the liquor terrible, and the music... well.... *How do they listen to that stuff?*

Late as it was, I wasn't ready to go home. So I figured I'd take a walk, wander the streets a little, then grab a cab and go to bed. That was a stupid thing to do. Chattanooga isn't the friendliest town at midnight in winter, but there I was. I ended up on the Walnut Street Bridge, freezing my ass off, staring down into the water, and... I was a little nervous.

I wasn't worried I might get mugged or anything. Far from it. I'm a big guy, and an ex-cop, and I was carrying a concealed Smith & Wesson M&P9 in a shoulder rig under my left arm. But there was something in the air that night, something other than the driving snow, and I could feel it. It made my skin crawl. Something I couldn't put my finger on.

I'd walked the few yards north on Broad, turned right on Fifth, then left on Walnut, and from there to the bridge, a pedestrian-only walkway across the Tennessee River to North Shore.

I was still on the south side, on the second span, leaning on the parapet looking west along Riverfront Parkway. I must have been standing there shivering for more than thirty minutes when I saw her. Well, I heard her first. She was on Walnut, running toward me, her heels clicking on the sidewalk. I recognized her. I'd seen her earlier, in the Sorbonne. She'd been sitting at the bar with two men, two tough-looking creeps, one tall and black with slicked back hair, the other one not so black, better dressed, smaller, and obviously the alpha. They were both wearing those shiny, quilted jackets. I'd wondered at the time what the hell she was doing there with them. She was out of their league by a mile: a classy, good-looking woman who looked as if she'd be more at home at the country club than at Benny Hinkle's sleazy dive.

She was maybe twenty-six or twenty-seven years old and wearing one of those little black dresses things that cling and stick to every curve. She had red hair. Not that gaudy, fiery orange kids seem to go for these days—a muted amber that was either her own or had cost more than most people earned in a week. But it was her face that grabbed you. She might have been right out of one of those glossy fashion mags, a face that could only have come from good breeding—wow, there's an old-fashioned term—and I remember thinking, *She's probably the wife or daughter of one of the movers and shakers up on the mountain.* Add the pair of five-inch black stilettoes and the white cashmere parka that could only have come from 5th Avenue or Rodeo Drive, and I knew immediately that she was no ordinary, working-class pickup.

So what's she doing here arguing with those two? I remember how I shook my head and stared at her legs. They went all the way up to her ears, and then some.

I didn't dwell on her for long. I was too wrapped up in my own workaday problems to give a damn, but there was something about her that caught my interest and wouldn't let go.

Now here she was in the wind and snow, running, frightened, looking back over her shoulder as if she were being chased. Then she tripped, stumbled, almost fell. I started toward her, but as soon as she saw me, she stopped. She put her hands to her mouth, looked desperately about her, then turned, ran to the rail, and started to climb.

"No!" I sprinted the few yards that separated us, but I was too late. She was on the rail before I could reach her. She looked wildly around, first along Walnut and then at me... and then she jumped. I dove the last couple of yards, my arms outstretched, and I managed to grab the collar of that fancy parka with both hands. I slammed into the rail. Man, was she heavy. I hung onto the fabric, hauled on it as hard as I could, but it wasn't enough. She simply threw her arms over her head, slipped out of it, and fell. I barely heard the splash over the noise of the wind howling through the ironwork overhead. I leaned over the rail and looked down. Nothing, just the white caps on the river some eighty feet below. She wouldn't last more than a few minutes in those icy waters, supposing she'd even survived the fall.

I took out my cell and dialed 911. There was nothing else I could do. I told the operator what had happened, gave her my name and location, and settled down on one of the bench seats to wait, the parka folded over my lap. I picked it up. It was heavy.

Okay, okay. I'm a nosy son of a bitch. But I'm a

private detective, and the temptation was just too much. I searched the pockets. I didn't find much. There was a set of keys to a BMW in one, and a pair of white cashmere gloves and an iPhone 6 in the other. I pulled down the zipper at the front, looked at the tag and inside of the collar: Neiman Marcus. In the inside pocket was a leather clutch, pale blue, with a snap closure at the top. It was unusual, obviously expensive, and a little larger than those handy little accessories most trendy young women like to carry. I opened it and rifled through the contents. *Jeez, $2,300 in hundreds, and God knows how much in fifties and twenties.*

I put the money back, fiddled some more, found three business cards—also expensive—and a key. An ordinary key, as far as I could tell. The cards read "Tabitha Willard." Her address? Her occupation? Nada. There was nothing on it other than the name and a phone number. I searched the purse and all of her pockets again, but again found no driver's license, no ID. Keys to a Beemer, but no license. That was strange.

By now, I could hear sirens coming, so I returned everything to the purse but one of the cards, which I slipped into my own overcoat pocket, and returned the purse to the inside pocket of the parka.

"What the hell have you done now, Starke?"

I might have known. It took only my name and a 911 call to attract the attention of the CPD in general, and Sergeant Lonnie Guest in particular. That fat bastard hated my guts and didn't care who knew it. He had since we were at the police academy together. He couldn't stand how tough it had been for him, and how easy for me. I always wondered how he'd made it through at all, much less past the final exam. Then I found out: the SOB was a cousin to the mayor. Hah, Even that didn't help him much. As soon as the cousin lost the election, Lonnie lost his support. He made sergeant eight years ago, just before the mayor left office. It was his honor's last official act, his way of getting back at the city for not supporting him. Lonnie's going nowhere in the department, has no chance of promotion. The dumbass can't pass the lieutenant's exam.

I looked up at him and smiled the smile I knew chapped his jaw.

"Not a thing, Lonnie. I just made the call. She went over the rail into the water. I managed to save her coat. Here you go." I tossed it to him. He caught it and scowled, first at the coat, then at me.

"You're trouble, Starke. Nothin' but trouble. You may have the rest of 'em flimflammed, but not me. We shoulda locked you away years ago. Tell me what happened."

"Nah. I'll wait till someone who knows what they're doing gets here. No point in spilling it all twice."

"You'll tell me, you arrogant son of a bitch. I'm first officer on the scene."

"So you are, Lonnie, so you are. Is that soup you have on your shirt?"

He looked down. I laughed. "Gotcha."

"Screw you, Starke, you piece of shit."

I looked at my watch, took out my phone, texted

Lieutenant Gazzara, and asked her to come on down. She would not be pleased.

"Suicide, Lonnie. She ran along Walnut like the devil was after her, spotted me, and hopped over the rail. Gone, Lonnie. Into the river. Suicide."

The phone vibrated in my pants pocket. I pulled it, unlocked it, and read the text.

"Now look, Lonnie, Kate Gazzara will be here in just a few, so why don't you go back to your cruiser where it's nice and warm, maybe take a nap, and I'll just hang out on this bench right here until she arrives."

"One of these days she ain't gonna be around to save your ass, Starke, an' I wanna be there when that happens."

"Yeah, well. In the meantime, you probably should make some calls, get some boats down there, and divers too. Not that they'll find anything in this mess." I looked up into the swirling snowstorm. It must have been blowing twenty miles an hour at least.

"Who the hell d'you think you are, Starke, givin' me orders? You just keep your trap shut and let us do our job, okay?" Then he did as he was told. He got on the phone and requested help from the Tennessee Wildlife river patrol and a dive team. Hah!

I grinned and settled down to wait, but not for long. She arrived less than five minutes later in an unmarked, and I was right; she didn't look happy.

"This had better be good, Harry, bringing me out in this weather. I'd been home less than ten minutes when you texted. I was on my way to bed." She sat down on the bench beside me.

I turned to look at her. She always amazed me. No matter what time of day or night, Kate always looked good: almost six feet tall, slender figure—ripped, I suppose is how you would describe it — she works out a lot. When she's at work, she keeps her long tawny hair tied back, but it was down just then, cascading around her shoulders, whipped by the wind. She has huge hazel eyes and a high forehead. She was wearing jeans tucked into high-heel boots that came almost up to her knees, and a white turtleneck sweater under a short, tan leather jacket. Even at one o'clock in the morning in the middle of a snowstorm, she looked stunning.

"So tell me what happened."

And I did. I told her the events of the past forty minutes, culminating with the girl taking a dive from the bridge. She didn't interrupt. She listened carefully to every word, nodding every now and then, and then she started asking questions.

"So, Harry...." She looked me in the eye. "Slumming again, huh? Why do you do it? Why do you go to places like the Sorbonne?"

"Just keeping my ear to the ground. It's in places like the Sorbonne where you learn things, not the fancy bars and restaurants."

"So... what did you find in her pockets?"

"Kate!" I tried to sound indignant, as if going through the woman's clothing was something I would never even think of doing, but she knows me better than I know myself. She tilted her head sideways and raised her eyebrows, an unspoken question.

"Okay," I sighed, and shook my head. "Yes, I glanced through her stuff." She rolled her eyes. "I hung onto this." I handed her the card. "There are two more just like it in her purse, wallet, whatever the hell it is. There's also a wad of cash, and a fob for a late-model BMW, the keyless type. No driver's license, though. Strange, huh?"

She nodded, fingered the card, turned it over, and looked at the back. "Hey! Sergeant Guest." She had to shout to be heard over the wind. "Bring that coat over here, will you please?"

Please? I'd have told the creep to get his fat ass over here, and quick, but I guess she's more lady than she is cop.... Nope, that ain't true. The lady's a lady, but she's all cop.

We both watched as the big sergeant leaned inside his cruiser and retrieved the parka. *Jeez, am I glad I haven't just eaten.*

He backed out of the car, then sauntered over. You ever seen a fat guy saunter? It's hilarious. The look on his face was a treat to behold too, when he dropped the coat on her lap. He looked like he'd just bitten into a lemon.

"Might be a good idea to search this light-fingered piece of garbage while you're at it, LT," he said with a smirk. "There's a whole lot o' cash in the wallet. Some of it might o' stuck to Starke here." He nodded down at me. I grinned back up at him.

"That's enough of that talk, Sergeant. How long before Wildlife and the divers get here?"

"They're on their way. Shouldn't be too much longer. I'll go wait in the cruiser, if it's okay with you."

"Yeah, go on. I'll call if I need you." She waited until he was back inside his car before she handed me the card. "I didn't give you that. If anyone asks, you stole it, right?"

I nodded. "Kate, the girl was frightened out of her mind. She seemed fine when I saw her earlier in the bar with two nasty-looking creeps. What the hell could have scared her like that? And what was she doing with those two? I've seen them around, but I don't know who they are. She was a lovely kid, Kate. I want to know what happened."

She didn't answer. She got to her feet, unfolded the parka, and let out a low whistle. "Whoa, cashmere, Neiman Marcus. This little number must have set her back at least four grand, maybe more. What I wouldn't give for one of these." She tucked the coat under her arm and opened the clutch.

"How much money is in here, Harry?" She rifled through the wad of bills.

"I'm not sure."

"Twenty-three hundreds, along with nine fifties and eight twenties: $2,910 in all. That's a lot of cash to be carrying around loose, especially into a place like the Sorbonne. What could she have been thinking?"

I nodded, but I didn't say anything. The divers were arriving on Riverfront Parkway, and there were blue lights flashing on the river; Tennessee Wildlife was here, too.

"Okay, Harry. You'd better take off and go home. Oh,

and, Harry, I know you're going to be looking into this; you can't help yourself. This time, though, that's probably a good thing, because we can't. It's a suicide, plain and simple; you said so yourself. We'll try to identify her, contact her next of kin, and all that. When we do, I'll call you, but you're right. From what you saw in the bar, there may be something more going on here. If so, we need to know. That's on you, Harry. I'll help, if I can, but stay out of trouble, and keep that goddamn gun in its holster. One more incident like the last one, and I won't be able to save you. You got that?"

She was talking about something I'd done a couple of months ago. I had to pull my weapon on a suspect. Turned out the guy was innocent. He didn't press charges, but the police weren't too happy about it. It wasn't the first time they didn't like something I did, though, and it surely wouldn't be the last.

"Got it. I'll start first thing in the morning." I looked at my watch. "Damn, it already is morning."

"Harry, if you find out anything, anything at all, call me, please. Otherwise, we'll stay in touch by text, right?"

I agreed. She folded the Neiman Marcus and walked slowly, head down, back to her car. As she passed Guest's patrol unit, she stopped, leaned in the window, and said something I didn't hear. Two minutes later, she hit the starter, did a three-point, and then sped off along Walnut, then turned left on East 4th, going east toward the hospital, going home, I supposed.

I didn't wait until morning. I walked off the bridge onto Walnut, then turned right and found a bench outside the aquarium. I took the card out of my pocket and punched the number into my phone.

"Yeah?" A male voice.

"Tabitha Willard, please?"

Click.

Son of a bitch. He hung up. I tried again, but there was no answer.

Okay, so it would have to wait until the city was awake. Bed seemed like a good idea.

I checked my watch. 1:15. I called a cab, then hunkered down in a doorway, out of the wind, and waited.

It was no more than a fifteen-minute ride to my place at that time in the morning. I paid the cabbie, slipped him an extra ten and wished him goodnight, what was left of it.

I threw my coat down on a chair in the kitchen, poured myself a stiff measure of Laphroaig Quarter Cask scotch and flung myself down on the sofa in front of the picture window. The wind and snow had slacked off almost to nothing, just a light breeze and a few flurries. A light mist covered the surface of the river, a soft gray blanket that swirled and undulated, turning the mighty Tennessee into a living thing. The view from my window was, as always, spectacular.

I lay there, staring out over the water, savoring the ten-year-old malt. My brain was in overtime. The events of the past few hours all came flooding back. Time after time, I saw the horrified look on the girl's face when she spotted me. I kept remembering the way she dropped, slowly turning end over end, splashing into the murky water far below. Was there anything else I could have done to save her? I was sure the question would haunt me for a very long time. There'd be no sleep for me tonight.

Geez, what a way to go.

———

Want to read the rest of the story? You can do so for just $0.99 or the equivalent in the country where you reside.

Just click this link

Made in the USA
Monee, IL
06 February 2021